DATE DUE   JUL 0 5

JAN 19 06			
9-18-10 S			
5-18-17 S			
GAYLORD			PRINTED IN U.S.A.

BLUE *Beyond* BLUE

Also by Lauren Slater

❋

OPENING SKINNER'S BOX

WELCOME TO MY COUNTRY

LOVE WORKS LIKE THIS

PROZAC DIARY

LYING, A METAPHORICAL MEMOIR

BLUE

Beyond

BLUE

EXTRAORDINARY TALES
FOR ORDINARY DILEMMAS

Lauren Slater

With illustrations by Stephanie Knowles

W. W. NORTON & COMPANY
NEW YORK ∗ LONDON

For information about permission to reproduce selections
from this book, write to Permissions, W. W. Norton &
Company, Inc., 500 Fifth Avenue, New York, NY 10110

Manufacturing by Quebecor World, Fairfield
Book design by Dana Sloan
Production manager: Amanda Morrison

Library of Congress Cataloging-in-Publication Data

Slater, Lauren.
Blue beyond blue : extraordinary tales for ordinary dilemmas /
by Lauren Slater.—1st ed.
p. cm.
ISBN 0-393-05959-6
1. Fairy tales—United States. 2. Psychological fiction, American. I. Title.
PS3619.L373B58 2005
823'.0108—dc22

2005005579

W. W. Norton & Company, Inc.
500 Fifth Avenue, New York, N.Y. 10110
www.wwnorton.com

W. W. Norton & Company Ltd.
Castle House, 75/76 Wells Street, London W1T 3QT

1 2 3 4 5 6 7 8 9 0

For Clara and Lucas
My Two

Contents

BLUE *Beyond* BLUE

Introduction

PERHAPS BECAUSE I am a psychologist and a writer, people have often asked me whether my writing is therapeutic. I used to say no. That's because I thought of therapeutic
things as soothing, salving, waterfalls and new age music,
massage and exercise. But if I expand the word therapeutic
to include any process in which the self's core conflicts and
fears and sufferings are engaged, any process that lays out
one's body or mind for revision and repair, then yes, I would
have to say my writing is therapeutic.

Writing is a fraught process, one which I approach with
trepidation, a process in which I dislike myself more often
than not, a process whereby I have to face the white page,
which is all my blanknesses, all the space I am afraid to
inhabit. Writing forces me to move between what I call the
inside world and the outside world. The inside world is one
where imagination resides, and the outside world is where

you need to cook your kids dinner. Moving between the two is uncomfortable for me, a process of disengaging and reengaging, only to disengage and reengage in the other direction, all the while never knowing if this time your access to one of these worlds will be blocked. Writing forces me into love, shows me that love is as moral as it is emotional. You love a story when you work on it even though it may not meet your expectations. You love a story and see it through even when it is born badly, bungled, crippled, or just plain ugly. Learning to love the ugly—by which I mean commit to it—is one of writing's great lessons, and I take it with me everywhere.

So yes, writing is therapeutic because no matter who you are or how you do it, chances are your own fears and shortcomings will find expression in the process. Equally important, the stories you generate will at once reveal to you your mind while offering up chances to change it. If one accepts the premise that lives are, among other things, coconstructed narratives—stories we tell ourselves, with family and friends, about who we are, how we came to be, why we are troubled, where we fail—then it is not difficult to also accept the premise that both articulating and revising these narratives can lead to productive change.

Narratives, of course, can take many forms; for one, some

are spoken and others are written. It is my belief that, for therapeutic purposes, the written narrative has a power that the spoken does not. Writing provides one with a literal record; it often forces one to wager a continual kind of coherence.

It is for these reasons that I, as a psychologist, have often used writing in my treatment of patients. I find it an especially useful tool when you have reached a certain comfort level, when the sessions descend into chitchat, when you've been meeting every week for too many months, and there are still ledges to be cleared, but you can't quite find them. Setting pen to paper will reveal those ledges, those hot spots and soft spots and strengths. When a patient sets pen to paper she is thrust lickety-split into her own white space, at which point she can transcribe what emerges, or create language that cradles her experience.

Narrative psychotherapy has a small but fervent group of followers; some would pinpoint its real beginning in the 1980s, when Michael White and David Epston published their influential book *Narrative Means to Therapeutic Ends*. Since that time narrative therapy centers have sprung up in places from Canada to Australia. Narrative therapy flourished with the postmodern belief that the world offered multiple meanings, multiple stories, one as good as the other, rightness being relative.

Epston and White saw narrative therapy as indebted to Michel Foucault, who famously said, "Knowledge is power." They discussed the sociopolitical implications of dominant cultural narratives and the tremendous power they wield, and they suggested that those who dare to challenge and change those narratives are performing a political as well as a personal act. Feminism is a ready example of such action: There was one dominant story of white women in which they were for the most part demure and hitched to their houses. Their reproductive anatomy and hormonal status destined them for a life of caretaking and made them moody and unpredictable. Feminism was about reimagining the story, recasting the central characters, questioning the story's central assumptions: Why was home, for instance, a less important sphere than work? Or war? Did hormonal shifts make a woman moody and unreliable, or did they, perhaps, supply a kind of richness? Slowly, stories began to change.

In actuality, narrative therapy is usually not practiced on a global scale. It is an intimate encounter between one writer and her page, one page and its audience, in this case the therapist. Central to the idea of narrative therapy is the issue of "externalization." One of the goals of narrative therapy is to separate the person from the problem, to give the problem its own personal existence that lives outside of the patient. By doing this, the patient then has the chance to step back and survey the scene with new perspective, to consider the relationship between himself or herself and his or her conflict. In doing so, patients come face to face with the subjugating language and plot points typically given to problems. In fact, such a relational but distanced stance often reveals the oppressive nature of much socially held descriptive knowledge and allows for the possibility of transformation.

Externalization requires the person to "objectify and to at times personify the problems that they experience as oppressive" (*Narrative Means to Therapeutic Ends*, by Michael White and Daniel Epston, W. W. Norton, p. 38). Once that has been accomplished, the person has the opportunity to cast him- or herself, as a character, in a new way, or to restate the problem, or to come up with an entirely new alternative, in which case previously excluded "facts" may now surface, and previously included "facts" may become peripheral and even insignificant.

Narrative therapy and its externalization of the problem can take many different forms. Epston and White use letters. Some narrative therapists will have their patients write their own eulogies, the first eulogy expressing what could currently be said about the person, the second eulogy expressing what the person hopes can be said of him or her at the end of life. The gap between the first and second eulogy in many ways contains the problem's externalization and methods of closing that gap are expressed in writing, the healing variable. Or in treating substance abuse, for example, a narrative therapist may ask the person to personify his craving, make it into a character, and then question it in new ways: Why are you here? What do you want? Of what are you afraid?

I believe fairy tales possess a special power in the role of narrative therapy. A fairy tale is often the starkest, cleanest utterance of our selves. By stating the problem in such a primitive form, patients can gain a purchase on it they might not have had before. Fairy tales are always, always symbolic, and, once we have created our symbols, we then have the opportunity to both modify them and more deeply understand their limitations. Fairy tales allow us, even force us, to think outside of conventional boundaries: What happens next? You have to imagine it.

Fairy tales offer us the opportunity for enchantment, for delight, states of mind often quashed by mental illness. Perhaps even more significantly, fairy tales, by insistently and consistently rendering plain objects in unexpected, magical ways, cause significant shifts in the mind of the reader, or writer. In fairy tales, a finger can become a key, a tree might talk. Entering such a world, the mind is disinhibited; it can see new possibilities, within the story and within the self.

Fairy tales also have important healing social implications. They may place us alone in the forest, but, at the same time, the telling of them links us to a whole history of humanity. We are not alone; this story has been told before; this is not a new quest, we are a part of something larger. Our lives are highly significant, the stuff of myths and magic; we are heroes, every one. The fairy tale, simply by its mere undertaking, forces a person to view his life with both a whimsy and a seriousness he may never have had before.

Several decades ago, Bruno Bettelheim wrote the influential book *The Uses of Enchantment: The Meaning and Importance of Fairy Tales*. He explored why fairy tales have power for children. He bemoaned the vacuosness of most children's literature and claimed that fairy tales were not only powerful tools for the transmission of culture, but also for helping children learn to master their fears, identify with the good, experience triumph over wayward nature, and face evil with strength. Bettelheim's interpretation of fairy tales themselves was largely Freudian, which in some sense limits his discussion. He occasionally too rigidly restricts himself to an analysis of drives and repression, thereby overlooking other interpretive possibilities. But his thoughts on the meaning these tales have for children, their potentially powerful pur-poses in instructing and healing, remain convincing.

What Bettelheim fails to stress, however, is that fairy tales were never intended solely for children. They were pieces of folklore passed down from one generation to the next. They were stories told by communities in trouble and not; adults listened, and still do, to Little Red Riding Hood or the Seven Ravens because the images, of being devoured and devouring, of a stomach filled with stones, of brothers becoming birds, the lonely loss of siblings, are not age-related themes. They are, truly, timeless.

As with children, adults need fairy tales too. They offer us the same opportunities to master fear, tussle with craving, and, most importantly, come face to face with a moral force. While adults can find these themes couched in the more sub-tle complexities of literary novels, stories, and essays, there is something about the stark polarization of fairy-tale char-acters, combined with their deeply evocative nature, that makes us, in reading them, or writing them, remember our own childhoods. And in returning to the place where the problem often began, these tales can become especially potent therapeutic tools. When you ask an adult to write or revise a fairy tale, you are asking him or her to head into the heat, where chemical changes and reactions take place.

Practically speaking, as a therapist, I have written fairy tales for my patients, tales that mirror what I see as their conflicts, and then asked them to find several different endings, or take one character and start a written dialogue with him or her about the story, or write a letter to a character, the wolf or Hansel shut up in his cage. I have asked families in conflict to try, each member, writing a fairy tale from an unusual point of view: The beleaguered daughter can take the role of the wicked mother/stepmother and try to tell the story from her point of view; the angry mother can explain to the passive father why it is that she is sending her children into the forest, and the role he has played in this decision. Similarly, the phobic patient can write as Gretel, who started out meek but ended as the leader.

In this way, patients are exposed to illuminations offered by both the process and the product of writing. As authors of their own experience, they confront the existential anxiety inherent in putting pen to paper and, having moved through this process, they then emerge with a story that offers the chance for revelation and transformation. I can think of no other therapeutic tool that gets quite so quickly to all the hearts of the matter.

In this book I have compiled my own fairy tales. Writing them has forced me to bear something out of blankness, and this is good; the tales have also revealed to me who I am, in part, at this point in time, each story a snap of the shutter, a piece of my mind now frozen in time.

Writing these stories has also been a social act; it has put me into dialogue with other fairy tales and stories in a process of cross-pollination that I have found meaningful. Other peoples' tales and stories have occasionally entered my consciousness as a part of my own lived experience, and in some cases challenged me to create something new from an inspiring image, a dilemma, a salient feeling. Writers to whom I am indebted include Aimee Bender, Barry Yourgrau, Yasuari Kawabata, and Karen Brenner.

I encourage clinicians, readers, and writers alike to use these stories in whatever ways they want, for pleasure, or for inspiration in their own writing, or as tools in a psychotherapeutic process. I hope these tales give rise to more tales. That would be my greatest wish: that they inspire someone as I was inspired by others, and in the process produce change. Everyone, absolutely everyone, has a tale to tell. And everyone, absolutely everyone, will have to revise it, only to revise it again. This is what, as a clinician practicing narrative psychotherapy, you try to help your clients do: create new plotlines for problem-saturated stories. But you don't need to be in therapy to get the therapeutic effect of writing, in all its scariness and pleasure. You can do it on your own, set pen to paper, see who talks back, learn to wish again or for new things, find your way through the forest, every word a bread crumb marking your passage from here to there, how you tore through the darkness, how you found something sweet. You can try it.

Blue Beyond Blue

1

THERE ONCE was a woman who had never had any children. This bothered her, and, as the years went by, the bother turned to grief. She lived alone, in a tidy house, while outside, in the fields, roses redder than crayons grew wild and thick. The woman liked to go for walks. She liked to pick flowers and see the pollen on her hands.

One day, while out walking, the woman came across a briar patch denser than any she had seen before, each enormous flower the size of a pink platter. These roses, strangely, had no thorns—their stalks were smooth and beaded with water—so the woman walked right into their thicket and there, lying on the ground in the shade, she saw a little egg.

"If I cannot have a child," the woman thought, "then perhaps I can at least have a small sparrow to keep me company." So she took the egg home with her, and put it on her windowsill, and then she waited for it to hatch.

Days passed and the egg, which started out as the size of a small speckled stone, did not hatch. Instead it just grew bigger, and by the end of the week it was as large as a melon, and strange scratching sounds were coming from inside it.

"This is obviously not a sparrow's egg," said the woman. "It must be an ostrich egg."

But after three weeks passed, and nothing had hatched, and the egg was as plump as a pumpkin, she thought, "Perhaps I have found some prehistoric creature, a dinosaur," and the woman grew scared.

The woman went to the town doctor. She explained her situation, and the doctor was so amazed that he rushed with her to her house.

Inside, the doctor looked for a long time at the giant egg. He took out his stethoscope and listened to its innards. He peered at its shell with his magnifying glass. He tapped at it with his little red rubber reflex hammer, all the while scratching his chin just like a learned man must.

At last he turned to the woman. His gaze was serious and direct. From his black bag he pulled a scalpel, but this was no ordinary scalpel. This had a blade as thin as hair, as sharp as Arctic wind, and its handle was made of carved bone. The doctor said, "I am giving you this scalpel as a gift, in light of what you have here. Wait until midnight, and then make a sideways slit in the shell, precisely four inches in length," he said, and with a marker he drew a line on the egg where she was to cut—at midnight.

The woman took the scalpel with its handle of bone. She felt scared. That evening, darkness came fast and definite, snuffing out the contours of the land, swallowing sounds, making the roses bloom black in the fields. The woman trembled. Waiting until midnight, she could not help but think of all the sins she'd committed in her life, small sins but sins nonetheless, and she had the terrible sense that the egg contained these things, and that she would slit it open to see the darkest heart of herself.

Midnight came. An animal howled and a tiny red Mars blistered the sky like a sore. The woman now no longer wanted to cut open the egg, but a strange force called compulsion—and its kinder cousin, curiosity—both of those propelled her. She made the small slit, just as the doctor had instructed. At first, nothing happened, but then some liquid oozed from the incision, and then came a little white leg wearing, of all things, a flip-flop, and then came a second white leg, wearing, of all things, a flip-flop, and then a torso struggled out, the shell cracking, a girl, maybe three, maybe four, pulling her head free last, and in her hands she held a clean white envelope, which she offered immediately to the woman.

The woman, awestruck, took the envelope and opened it. There was a note, folded up. She unfolded the note. She saw:

$$==0^*))))$$
$$+++\%!\$no^\wedge$$

The woman squinted harder at the gibberish. It stayed just as it was, gibberish. Then she squinted at the little girl. "Who are you?" The woman said.

"I am your daughter," answered the girl.

Now, the woman could not believe this. It was just too good to be true. The darkness, it turned out, had augured not sin, but bounty, as darkness sometimes does. The woman just stood there and blinked and blinked. She said, "Show me your hands."

The little girl showed her her hands, which were, each one, five-fingered and perfect. The woman said, "Walk to the door and back," which the girl did, on two feet, wholly human, and then the woman said, "Pinch a piece of your skin, as hard as you can," which the girl did, until she cried out in pain, and the woman said, "Stop! Stop! I hear how you are human," and she took the girl to her, and tasted her tears.

2
—

YEARS WENT BY. Mother and child were happy. They grew root vegetables and played harmonicas. They slept in two beds pushed side by side, and together they watched the moon move through the month, now plump as an egg, now a silver sliver, and, over time, the girl forgot where she was from, and believed she belonged wholly to her mother. And, over time, the mother, although she never forgot where the girl was from, believed the girl belonged wholly to her. Sometimes, when the girl slept, the mother anxiously, but oh so gently, checked the girl's toes and tongue, to make sure she was, well, a girl, and always her toes and tongue, plus everything else, looked normal.

The only thing that was not normal was the girl's voice, but in this instance abnormal was not bad, it was good. The girl had the most beautiful voice, like a piccolo was inside her, and when she sang all the birds stayed still in the trees and listened.

And so the years went by and mother and child slept side by side and kissed each other constantly and the woman had happiness at last. And then, during the summer of the girl's twelfth year, just as she should have begun to grow breasts, something very disconcerting happened.

The woman noticed, growing not from her front, but from her shoulder blades in back, where the girl could not see, two tiny feathered mounds.

At first the mounds were so tiny they were more like downy patches, but day by day they sprouted and the woman was always trying to get a good look at them, and the daughter, who was twelve and becoming irritable, said, "Stop pressing on my back every other minute, would you?" and the woman said, "I am just trying to make sure your shirt is buttoned."

The daughter had no idea about the wings.

At night now, alone, the mother grieved. She recalled how, long ago, when she had slit open the strangest shell to find a tiny child whom she had come to think was of her, from her, she had known it was too good to be true. Her girl was not of this world. The mother cried. She got up one night, tiptoed across the creaking floorboards, and opened a locked box, where she had saved the scalpel and the mysterious letter. She unfolded the letter again, after all these years, and stared at its mysterious message.

$$==0^*))))$$
$$+++\%!\$no^\wedge$$

and still she could make no sense out of it. She knew nothing of this written language, but what she did know was that if her daughter grew wings, as her body seemed to want so badly to do, then she would soon fly away from her, for one has wings only if one wishes to fly, and fly far, and then the woman would be all alone again, in a tidy house, with the wild roses growing in an abundant profusion.

The woman picked up the scalpel. Time had not blunted its blade, and the carved-bone handle had a pearly glisten. The daughter slept soundly. A white owl flew by the window, its wingspan massive, its eyes alarmed. The woman went toward her sleeping girl, drew back the covers like a nurse draws back a bandage to expose the flesh, and then there they were, the wings, two budding structures of piped bone and scaly feathers, not yet detected by their owner. The mother lowered the scalpel and then, in one swift swish, cut off the left wing, and then in one swift swish cut off the right wing, and the daughter did not awaken, but in her dreams she felt a searing pain, and saw birds falling from above.

The next morning, when the daughter awoke, she had a fever and her back badly hurt. "What is wrong with my back, what is wrong with my back?" the child called out, and her tongue was swollen, her eyes gone glazed, and the mother, frantic, pressed cool washcloths to her forehead. Had she killed the girl? Would her daughter die?

For six days the child thrashed and moaned and then, on the seventh day, she was suddenly, remarkably, better. Glow crept back into her cheeks. She ate some sweet potatoes. She climbed out of bed and said, "Everything feels fine, except these spots on either side of my back," and she stood before the mirror and, twisting around, caught a glimpse of where the wounds were.

"What has happened to my back?" the daughter cried. Any wounds would be odd enough, but these wounds were odder still. Where the mother had cut were two slits, each one miraculously healing in a strip of shiny gold.

"Why do I have that funny color on my back?" the daughter said.

The mother searched in her head for an explanation. Of course she wasn't going to say, "Well, dear girl, while you were asleep I came at you with a scalpel because I didn't

want you to leave me," so instead she did what many mothers do, she told a sort of half-truth, designed to protect both
parties. She said, "You had a great fever and a golden rash for
six days; you almost died, you almost left me, but now you
are well, except for these minor markings, which do not matter. What matters is that we are together again, and will be
together forever."

The girl, who was twelve and did not take anything
about her body as minor, said, "I will never wear a bathing
suit with these things on my back." She wept as though she'd
been gored, which in a way she had. The mother rocked the
girl and said, "Shhh, shhhh, it will be okay." The mother did
not feel okay. Her heart was heavy. She loved her girl, but,
until now, she had not known that love could be so sharp.

3

THE GIRL GREW UP and grew beautiful and then, one day, fell
in love with an acrobat. The mother said, "How will he support you, doing flips?" and the girl said, "We need very little," and, indeed, the mother knew this to be true, for she
herself needed very little, except the love of this girl, who
was leaving her now, for a man in a red stretch suit.

The girl and the acrobat planned their wedding for an April day. The acrobat was anxious to get through the ceremony, because every time he tried to undress his lover she said, "No no, wait until we are married," when in truth marriage was not the issue. She was embarrassed by her back, with its golden scars. On the actual wedding day, there were many feelings and fears experienced by many people. The girl felt frightened, for very soon she would have to take off her clothes and show her imperfect body, but she also felt excited, because she loved the acrobat. The acrobat felt anticipation. The girl's mother, who had helped plan the wedding, felt a deep melancholy, but also a sense of pride, for her daughter had grown to be beautiful and intelligent.

The wedding progressed with music and champagne, and then the bride and the bridegroom danced together, and then, as was the custom, everyone else had a dance with the bride. The officiator said, "It is now dusk. We have celebrated the union of this man and woman for a full joyous day, but we, as is our custom, cannot come to closure unless every man has danced with the bride. Is there any man here who has not had a chance to dance with the bride?"

And then, from out of the sky, a huge black bird appeared, circling slowly, dropping lower, calling, *Keeyaa keeyaa*, as though his heart were breaking. The wedding party hushed.

The men stepped back instinctively, and the bird, black as obsidian, shiny as mica, revolved just over their heads. The girl, as though under a spell, walked into the center of the crowd, and she made gentle waving motions with her arms on the ground while the bird made gentle waving motions with his wings in the sky, and the girl opened her mouth and the most beautiful sounds came out, sounds of grief on this, her wedding day—the strangest song.

4
—

MOST THINGS—but not all—change with time. The girl's grief was, in some sense, short-lived, because as soon as she was back in the arms of the acrobat, she felt an enveloping safety. On the other hand, the girl had a deeper grief, a grief that had been in her body ever since the night she'd lain asleep, scalpeled.

The girl and the acrobat went away to the acrobat's home at the outskirts of the village. The wedding party dispersed. The mother stood for a long time waving her handkerchief in farewell, and the mother thought, "Many years ago I tried to stop my child from flying away, but she has flown away anyway, because that is destiny, which cannot be cut."

The mother went home, back to her house. She was alone again. But she also knew her girl would come visit her, and so she was not wholly alone.

Even though years had passed since the night she had cut into her daughter, the mother had never been able to forgive herself for what she'd done. It was as though she had a stone in her stomach.

The girl, meanwhile, entered the acrobat's cottage, and the acrobat began, very gently, to peel off her clothes. The girl grew frightened. "No no," she cried, and the acrobat said, "Shush-sh, hush-sh," and he removed her clothes so gently and with such skill that she felt little twitches in her body, twitches that were part fear and part excitement.

And at last, when her clothes were fully removed, and she stood naked, and he walked around her, at last he saw the golden scars. "What are these?" he said.

"I don't know," the girl whispered. She hung her head. "I had some rash when I was little, they're ugly, I know," and she tried to hide herself by backing up against the wall.

"No no," said the acrobat. "They are beautiful," and he meant it. He turned her on her stomach on the bed and, standing over her, he kissed the scars with so much genuine passion that two fully formed wings burst upon her back, as though they'd just been waiting beneath the skin for a welcoming committee.

"What's that?" the girl cried, her face in the pillow. "What has come up upon my back?" and the acrobat, a man who loved adventure, who cherished the gaps between solid stones, who liked nothing better than to enter the air of utter possibility, said, "My love. You have wings! Those scars were hiding wings!" and there was delight in his voice.

The girl stood up and walked over to the mirror. "Oh my god," she said, for the wings were not diminutive. They were huge, white and gray, and she could make them flap. "What has happened to me?" she whispered.

"You are part angel," the acrobat said, and he came toward her and kissed her on the mouth, and they made love and afterward he said, "You are more beautiful to me now than ever."

And, indeed, the girl felt, well, she felt for the first time, if not beautiful, then somehow *right*. She didn't understand why the wings felt so thoroughly comfortable. She didn't understand why she felt so strangely complete, so at peace. She realized that for a long, long time, there had been an ache in her body, a place of muffled pain, and now it was resolved, and her spirit felt light and yellow.

She sang and flew around the hut. The acrobat practiced flips and dips. They were an excellent couple.

The only thing was, the girl was too afraid to go home and visit her mother. "What will she think when she sees I have WINGS?" the girl wondered. "She will think it's the strangest thing, and I won't know how to explain it," but the girl missed her mother. A few times, she put on a big shirt sewn of sailcloth, her wings stuffed inside, and walked back to her mother's hut, but each time she got close, a dread filled her, and there was a terrific ache in her shoulder blades, the feeling of something slicing something off, and in her mind's eye, a drop of bright rich blood, and before she could help herself, she was whisked by her self straight up into the sky, and, flapping fast, went back to her second home.

5

Now, it just so happens that the mother, one day, was watching by the window and saw her daughter approach the house in a big white shirt, and then saw her daughter sail into the sky, the wings flapping fast and free. And the mother said, "She is afraid to come home to me. Her true body has triumphed and she doesn't want me to know." When the mother saw that the daughter's true body had triumphed, she did not feel dread or disappointment; she too felt a kind of yellow lightness, a certain lifting of the sodden spirit, because, well, for the mother, she saw how the wings were not only for leave-taking, but for return, and that pleased her. Even more importantly, the mother saw how the daughter's body was fluid in the sky, how she cartwheeled among clouds. She was a good mother with a great though imperfect love for her girl; in the end, it was love that won out, no question, it was love, as she watched the girl skim across the sky, and the mother's mouth opened into a joyful oh. Oh.

The mother went over to the locked box where, for all these years, she'd stored the scalpel and the mysterious note the girl had had with her in the egg. She put these things in a basket and set off to the acrobat's hut. On the way she found feathers scattered here and there across the ground, and she knew instinctively which feathers came from the body of her girl, which from the bodies of other birds.

When she got to the acrobat's hut, she knocked on the door and the girl opened it. "You don't have to hide from me," the mother said immediately. She touched her daughter's cheek. She remembered how she had waited, waited in the darkness for the egg to hatch, how she had seen the small white leg step over the cliff of cracks, how she had tasted her tears. "I know all about your wings," said the mother. She paused. "I have known about them for years."

"But I only just got them a few weeks ago," said the girl.

"May I come in?" asked the mother.

The girl stepped back to let her mother in. They sat together at the table. The mother, then, told her the entire story, how she had been born from an egg found in the woods, how, at twelve, she had started growing wings, how the mother, afraid of losing the girl to foreign lands, to the sky itself, had cut them off, and the mother cried in the telling, cried with a handkerchief wadded at her mouth, and the daughter cried too, and said, "Shhh, shhhh," and they kissed and tasted each other's tears.

"I did it because I loved you so much," said the mother, "and I did not understand how love can be so sharp."

"It is so strange," said the daughter, "because the very same hands that cut the wings from my body cradled the egg, birthed me, everything is always like that."

"Like what?" the mother said.

"Kindness and cutting, they're all mixed up together."

"Yes," said the mother.

"Yes," said the daughter, and then they ate some scones.

And then the mother gave to the daughter the scalpel she

had long ago used to both birth her and hurt her, plus the mysterious folded note that she had had with her in the egg. "This scalpel," said the mother, "can bring life or break life; either way, it has great power. This note," said the mother, "may be gibberish or may be genius, I have no idea."

The daughter thanked the mother for the presents and put them away in the medicine chest, and life went on. She forgot about the presents, and she never read the note. She visited her mother three times a week and her mother grew a garden of eggplants and roses, and sea-green cucumbers that were so fat and healthy she sold them for an excellent price. Three years later, the girl got pregnant and there was great rejoicing all around. When it came time for delivery, the girl lay on her side and pushed and pushed, and the midwife said, "I see the head! I see the head!" and the acrobat wept, peering up into the tunnel that was his wife, and then out came the sphere of what they thought was the head but of course was really an egg.

Everyone was quiet. The egg lay there on the bed. The girl, panting, got up and went to the medicine chest, and now took out the note and the scalpel. She cut just as her mother had described to her, a four-inch slit on the surface of the egg, and she reached her hand in and pulled out a baby boy, who would, under the influence of time and testosterone, grow his own magnificent wings. Everybody understood that.

The girl, kneeling on the bed by bloody rags, her hair in a stream of sweat, opened the note from so long ago. It was written in the language of birds, which felt utterly familiar to her. The note said:

$$==O^*))))$$
$$+++\%!\$no^\wedge$$

Otherwise interpreted as (and she said it aloud):

> *I am yours*
> *On loan from time*
> *And the sky*
> *So please give me back to*
> *The blue beyond blue*
> *As all good parents must do*

And then the new baby boy let out a bellow, took his first breath, and began straightaway to grow up.

Placebo

T HE WOMAN was rich, but with many pains. She had pains in each of the five fingers on her left hand and each of the five fingers on her right hand. Her heels hurt her all the time, as did her tongue, her eyes, and her mouth.

The woman had many pains, but she was rich. Her town was rich. Every house had a high roof and a garden, but the woman could love none of it, because of her discomfort.

At last the woman went to the doctor. The doctor said, "Stick out your tongue," and then he said, "Stick out your heel," and then he said, "Stick out your head," and even after all that, the doctor could find nothing wrong with the woman.

So the doctor said, "There is nothing wrong with you, woman. Go home, and enjoy your garden."

And so she did. But her pain was with her all of the time.

The woman went back to the doctor. He checked her heel and her tongue and her head, and, this time, also her liver and other assorted organs, but every part of her was healthy and so he said, "Go home."

At home the woman lay in her bed. Servants tiptoed in and out of the room, carrying tea trays and tablets. Her husband came to her and lay cool cloths across her forehead. Months went by and at last, when her husband could stand it no longer, he took her back a third time to see the doctor.

The doctor, not knowing what to do, went into a secret room behind his office. There, he mixed sugar with water, patted the concoction into pills, and then brought them to the woman.

The pills were pretty pills. Like little bits of snow, or expensive crystals, they glittered in the doctor's palm.

"These pills," the doctor said, "have been sent to me by Dr. Franz Horwiggien, the eminent German physician, and they are very, very expensive, and they are known to cure every ill."

"How much?" asked the husband.

The doctor thought. Here was a dilemma. The pills were nothing but sugar from his breakfast table and water from his tap. Two cents. At most three. But people want to make a profit. He thought two million. He thought three. He looked at the ailing patient. He looked at her husband. The doctor sighed. He said, "The pills cost nothing unless they are successful. If they are successful, then I will charge you a fee."

The ailing woman and her husband thanked the doctor and went home. Once at home, they lay the pills on a saucer, and then the woman took them. Just as the doctor had instructed, she put two on her tongue and swallowed.

And what happened? Within one-two-three seconds, yes three seconds, she felt astonishingly well. Her heel, that bothersome heel, was fine and flexible, her tongue without ache, her head clear as a glass goblet.

"These pills," the woman whispered to her husband, "these pills are miracle pills." And that night, for the first time, she enjoyed the peals of the church bells, the dark ravens and owls filling all the trees.

She slept soundly, on a white embroidered pillow, and her dreams were all of crystals, snow, sweet pieces drifting down.

The doctor, meanwhile, could get no sleep. "Two million, three million," he kept thinking. "Did the pills work?" he kept thinking. "Franz Horwiggien," he kept thinking, even though there was no such man. The doctor had all he could ask for in life, but most often all is not enough, and this is the real sickness at the heart of every human.

In the morning, he called the ailing woman. "Oh no," she said, "I'm not ailing anymore. Your pills have cured me. Your pills are miracle pills. I must take them every day. You must give me a steady supply. And by the way, how much do we owe?"

"Three million," the doctor said, his voice low. "I mean," he said, "I mean two million."

The husband went back to the doctor and paid him two million, pronto, in cash. The woman, meanwhile, dressed in all her finery and went out about the town, exclaiming to everyone about the new miracle cure.

She told Goody Harrisburg, who was also rich and lived in a mansion. She told Mistress Feinstein and the eminent Master Silverstein, an attorney who also owned an island. And every one of these people, plus all the others to whom she spoke, limped or dragged or galloped on horseback or spilled out of shiny cars, right at the doctor's doorstep, because as soon as they heard about the miracle cure, they realized they too had the illness.

The doctor charged two million per pill and within ten minutes he was richer than all his rich patients. He gathered so much cash that the bills filled every room in his modest house, and so he could no longer use the rooms, and instead he slept cramped in a corner in the hall.

The doctor began to feel ill. His head hurt from the hard floor, his legs seized with cramps. His beloved dog ran away.

The doctor's plants died, because they could not see the sun for all the paper money piled by the windows.

During the day, the doctor sat hunched in his dark kitchen and made his pills. He had to work hours to fill the demand. They were not hard to make, but they took time, because each tablet he shaped by hand, so some were like crystals, others a sugary brooch, a white orchid, an opaque pearl, they were beautiful pills, but lies, every one, and the doctor felt sick in his heart.

The doctor thought he should stop his pill-making practice, but he could not. Something just drove him on. "People need my pills," he thought, but that was not it.

Years went by like this and the town prospered, but the doctor didn't. The doctor grew thin. In the nights he woke up and kept having to count his cash. His eyes glittered like a racehorse's eyes, and he grew a rangy beard. The towns-people became worried. "If our doctor dies," they said to each other, "who will give us such beautiful pills, such sweet, miraculous molecules? We could never make them ourselves."

And so the townspeople pooled all their money together and sent a letter to the most famous physician in the entire world, Dr. Spockle of the Carolinas, begging him to come and examine their ailing town physician.

Dr. Spockle said yes, he would come. He came in a jet. He

landed his jet right on the town doctor's overgrown lawn and paraded down the steps with his stethoscope shining on his chest, and the town doctor was just overwhelmed. Dr. Spockle was a genius. Dr. Spockle had six degrees from Harvard, five from Yale, and four from Princeton. He had discovered cures for ailing livers, hearts, gallbladders, and colons. The whole town came out and gathered to watch the meeting of these men. The rich woman who originally started this story introduced Dr. Spockle to the beloved town doctor by saying, "We were all in pain until his brilliant pill preparation saved us, and now he is wasting away, and we are in fear for all of our lives."

Dr. Spockle took the town doctor inside his house, where there was some privacy, and examined his heel, his tongue, his head, and could find nothing wrong. But he was a wise doctor, and instead of saying, "There is nothing wrong," he said, "You have probably never heard of tin tin disease, because I have just discovered it and," he said, his voice sinking into a whisper, "I have just been told I will be awarded the Nobel Prize for my findings."

"Oh," said the town doctor, his eyes sunken but wide with admiration.

"You have tin tin disease," Dr. Spockle said, "but luckily

we have a treatment. It's not a cure, mind you, but a treatment to reduce cramping and general misery and mental confusion stemming from overactive cell receptors in the brain."

"Of course," said the town doctor. He was just a town doctor and knew little of overactive cell receptors in the brain, and he was very impressed, not to mention demented from his business pursuits.

The famous Dr. Spockle turned away, then, and out of his black bag he pulled a bottle filled with molasses. "Take a teaspoon of this every day until you have finished the preparation. Then you will need no more. You will not be one hundred percent well, but you will be well enough to sleep on a bed, mingle with friends, and stretch your cramping legs."

"How much do I owe you," asked the town doctor, "for this special medication?"

Now, Dr. Spockle knew the situation. He knew of the rooms stuffed with money, the incredible profitable pursuit, and even though he was rich enough to own a jet and six pink sailboats, he too wanted more, which is the sickness at the heart of every human. And so he said, "You owe me seven trillion nine hundred and thirty-four dollars and ninety-nine cents," which was, incredibly, just the amount the doctor happened to have in all the rooms of his house.

The doctor swallowed the brown thick medicine. He stood by a tree in his yard as tractors and forklifts came to take away the money. As his rooms emptied, as from beneath the green piles he saw again the beloved blankets on his bed, his sturdy dresser with its scalloped handles, his windows giving him the sun each morning, the tea-stained sky, the rain and clouds, as he saw these things appear, his heart lifted. The cramps in his legs just went away. "Dr. Spockle makes good medicine," he said to himself, and he went back inside his house, and he started to feel fine again, and his dog came back, and he shaved his rangy beard.

Night after night, now, the moon is large and healthy. The moon is plump and rosy, and the grasses whisper in the wind. The doctor makes his medicine—sugar and water, each pill shaped more intricately than the next. In this way, he keeps the town healthy. He gives them his gifts, and as he does, over the years, he sees he is not so much a man of science, but of art.

As for the money, the doctor decides to charge what he should, enough for food and water plus the occasional extras. But as the years go by, something strange happens; he sees he needs fewer and fewer extras, because he becomes very absorbed in his work. He is a sculptor now, and some of his pills become just so beautiful that he cannot give them away. Instead he places them on his mantel, intricate lilies of sugar, a silver seahorse, a bird in midcall, its white beak open, its neck thrust up, so elegant and muscular that all who see it draw in a breath, and feel fine.

My Girlfriend's Arm

M Y GIRLFRIEND wanted to marry me, but I don't do marriage, so we broke up. We were sitting in a crowded city park. She said, "You're just so scared," and I said, "I know," and then we both cried. "Close your eyes," she said, and she put her fingers on my lids and pressed them down. I heard her rustling about. I felt her lay something in my lap. A great sleepiness came over me, and when I finally opened my eyes, my girlfriend was gone, but in my lap lay her arm, which she had obviously given me as a goodbye gift. There was a note with the arm. The note said, "Not for keeps. I'll be back for it in two weeks."

And so there I was, sitting on a bench in the midst of a busy city, and I felt acute embarrassment. I tucked the arm under my coat, its hand right over my heart, and my heart thrilled. My blood beat fast. Night came. I didn't move from the bench. Under the cover of darkness I laid the arm across my lap. It wasn't stiff. I could bend the fingers, which I did with my mouth, and then the elbow too, so the arm assumed a coquettish pose. From the grocery store behind me I heard people talking; they were talking, as usual, about disasters. There were wildfires burning and smoke would enter the city soon; I didn't care. People drifted from apartment buildings, hosed down their walkways and their flat ranch roofs. The air smelled of wet cement. I finally stood and walked home. I cradled her the whole way there.

WE STOOD in the entrance to my dark apartment. Then I held up her hand and she turned the doorknob for me. She soaped me in the tub. Truth be told, I liked the arm better than its owner. In its plump rounded flesh I could see the entire body—the entire being—of the woman, without having to bear her whole weight. I wondered if the arm would start speaking to me. It was coated on the top with the finest threads of hair. I laid it on the bed. Shadows pooled in the bent elbow. I lowered my lips and drank in that darkness.

The following days were sweet. The arm was an excellent companion. The arm didn't want to marry me. The arm let me lie silently and stare at the ceiling, and never once did it say, "What's wrong?" I didn't have to talk if I didn't feel like it, but if I did feel like it I could talk. What little I said seemed to delight the arm, as its palm would smile when I spoke of certain things, and, also, a kind of light would fill its length.

I am a man of many moods and dimensions. What I liked about the arm was its simultaneous specificity and genericness, all wrapped up in one. For instance, if I wanted a certain kind of familiar comfort, it was easy enough for me to see in the arm its owner, to touch its skin and recall the skin of the owner, which was rosy in some places, pale in others, which had a certain curved softness to it, and a smell of shampoo and sweat. Thinking of these things, I could lie side by side with the arm on the bed, and it was as if we'd never separated.

In different moods, though, the arm could take on different characteristics. Sometimes I imagined it belonged to a woman twenty years older than I, a woman with a raspy voice and sharp high heels who would tell me just what to do. Other times, I saw it belonging to a teenager, or a twelve-year-old girl, with the barest nick for a navel. All of this delighted me. The light coming through my slatted shades seemed to alter the arm's appearance; its nails grew, and some days I filed them, painted them, the lacquer thick and copper.

Two weeks passed, and I recalled the owner would be

back for her arm. Only if I agreed to marry her would she agree to let me keep her arm, and I simply couldn't do it. Marriage is essentially a contractual unidimensional state, a state bound by expectations scripted in advance of the relationship, and I am something—call it slippery, or improvisational—I am something else. I realized I was in a bind. I could not marry her, but nor could I bear to part with this perfect companion. So I escaped. I left my apartment in the smoke-filled city, and, with the arm, *my* arm, I rented a cabin in the woods.

There we lived. For a good long time.

I took up hunting—what else does one do in the woods?—and skinning too. With practice it got so I could skin an animal expertly, tugging its hide from its body like a thick wool sock. And sometimes, sleeping next to the arm, I dreamt I killed an animal, and removed its flesh to find it was made of pure pearl beneath, the bones nacreous and tough. One day, I shot a baby deer. I felt bad about that; it was a mistake. But so long as it was dead, I would eat the meat. I cut the deer open and inside its belly I found a gold band.

I brought the band home and put it on her hand. Then, two hours later, I took it off. She didn't mind this back-and-forth one bit, and I felt so free I finally left the band on, and we slept that way, side by side, her ring finger resting on my cheek.

The next day, just as the sun was rising, I heard a knock at the cabin door. A terror—that's all I can say—a terror suffused me. Slowly, slowly, I went toward the door and opened it. It wasn't the owner. It was, instead, a leg, in a high heel, a leg I didn't recognize, smoothly shaved and shapely. It minced over to the bed and laid itself below the arm. It kicked off its own shoe. Thereafter, every day, another piece of a person showed up, and eventually my claustrophobia came back, because I realized the arm had turned against me; it was assembling itself into a whole human being, whom I would have to reject, and then I'd be left with nothing but my solitude. Solitude, I thought, could be a kind of company. Solitude can have weight and shape. There it is, in the corner, by the closet.

Another arm arrived, and then a breast. Soon enough I realized these parts were not, in fact, from a single individual; they were from many different women. The first breast to come was black, the second fair and freckled. The legs were not the same length. The head, when it finally knocked at my door, was empty of everything, just a sphere with hair and ears and holes in its face. I knew what would happen next. Sure enough, the eyes arrived like little presents, one blue and one brown, lying at my doorstep, blinking. The eyes floated in, and, as with all the other parts, assumed their rightful place, and now the woman watched me.

I tried to think of this development as delightful, a thoroughly postmodern pastiche of a being, but I couldn't avoid the truth for long. These were obviously all body parts loaned to men in similar situations as mine—lost parts that were angrily seeking their center again. I realized that many men the world over had the same secret desires as did I, and that just as many women loaned them their limbs, abettors. At last, one morning, I opened my front door to find the mouth, a rosebud on the ground, with teeth inside.

I slept, that night, on the couch. When I woke up, the completed woman was watching me from the bed. She seemed to fill the whole space; her smell was everywhere; she was fundamentally unclean. She was mulatto, mismatched, and she leaned over the side of the mattress and spit. Then, from behind her ear, she pulled a cigarette, lit a match on her tooth, and sat back, smoking and watching me. I couldn't stop sweating.

At last she came forward and blindfolded me. "We're going to play a little trust game," the woman said. I felt, suddenly, syrupy with submission. She blindfolded me and led me around. She took me outdoors. We came to the edge of what I knew to be a high cliff. She stood behind me, her hands on my shoulders. She said, "So Seamus," even though I'd never told her my name. "What's your name?" I whispered, the wind whipping around me, the sound of loose scree falling into the gorge.

She didn't answer me. Instead, her grip tightened on my shoulders. I felt the cold space of air; I felt her hurl me into it; I felt the opposite of crowded; I was winded, breathless, on the brink of something much too big. I gasped, pitched forward into black and blueness, and then, just as I felt myself start to fall, at the very last second, she snatched me back, hugged me, hard, against her chest.

We stood together, embracing on the gorgeous flat ground. Although I couldn't see—the blindfold—I could hear her heart, so steady. I could feel her breath, moving me. *Hold me tight, oh hold me tight,* was just about all I could think.

"Do you want to blindfold me now?" she said, her lips at my ear.

"No," I said, "I'm happy here."

And I was.

—Inspired by Yasuari Kawabata

Morphed

I ONCE HAD a bottle in which I kept my husband. It was
made of green glass. I found him in there one afternoon,
shrunken like a salted slug, his knees drawn up to his chin.

I said, "Jack."

He didn't answer me. He wouldn't even look at me
through the glass. I expect eye contact from a person, at the
very least. "I love you, Jack," I said, but the truth was, I
didn't love him, not anymore. The past years had been bad.
His inventions were a bust; his stocks had gone south; he was
a failure. So I took a rubber stopper from the kitchen drawer,
and corked him in this miniature world.

It didn't take me long—maybe only minutes—to discover
how much better our lives could be with my husband in that
bottle. It was outfitted splendidly with a tiny bed, a miniature rocking chair, and a kitchen table on which sat the
smallest hunk of ham. All through the spring and summer

my husband stayed there. He spent hours reading the newspaper and talking on a doll-sized telephone, business calls I
assume, an effort to reverse his fortune. It didn't work. Sometimes he cried, and it was so much easier to see a tiny man
cry than a big one. I could comfort him; I could place the
bottle in the sink and rock it gently on warm waves, and
eventually he would sleep. He said, "Sue, you are good to
me," and I have to admit, I agreed. I felt my own superior
strength, and, perhaps even better, the particular character
of my husband's weaknesses changed. In short, his failures—
which had once loomed so large for us—now seemed incon-
sequential. They were not the failings of a man, but of a child
whom I could care for. Because of the bottle, I came to love
my husband once again.

Time passed, and we were living in harmony, although
my husband cried quite a bit. He was emotional. I kept the
bottle on the windowsill in our bedroom where in the nights
it emitted a faint buzz. Sometimes I would wake up, deep in
the darkness, and see my husband in a bell of light, holding
a tiny red train or a stapler the size of the tip of my thumb.
I never knew where he got these objects, or what they meant.
Once, when I woke up, a full moon was shining on him; he
practically pulsed with light, and I said, "Jack, what are you
doing in there?" but he was busy; he wouldn't tell me. He had

a hammer, some nails. Head bent, he seemed to be making something I knew would never count for anything.

I won't deny it, Jack had times of deep depression in his bottle, times when he would just lie on his bed and stare at the green glass ceiling, or drum his fingers on the prismed walls. Ta-dum ta-dum ta-dum. I liked that sound. Despite his sadness, or maybe even because of it, I count these years as good ones in our marriage. With him in his confinement, I went out and got myself a job. I made a lot of money, and I invested it wisely. I exercised my green thumb so twining plants climbed the walls of our living room, their leaves large and oily. I took singing lessons and discovered my lungs are capacious, and sometimes, in the mornings, getting ready for work, I'd do an aria and find birds with wet wings crowding the sills, listening.

Years passed. Jack settled into a strange sort of peace. Often he appeared deep in thought, staring at the world through his walls of windows. Tiny books and bits of balsa wood, buttons and doll-sized golden pens cluttered his surroundings. There were whole days when he would write madly. He took up painting and then the violin. At first his music was whiny and unsteady, but over time he mastered that miniature instrument; he could play Handel and Wagner, Beethoven and Brahms, moving the bow with a flourish, his elbow racing back and forth, the velvet pad tucked under his chin. It irritated me, and I couldn't say why.

And then this happened. I came home from work one day, shortly after my husband's forty-fourth birthday. He was playing *Requiem for the Dead*. I sat by the bed and watched him. When he was done, he tapped on the glass and said, "Sue, it's time I got out of here."

I felt panic. "Whyever would you leave?" I said. "You have your whole world in there, and our marriage is so harmonious."

"What kind of marriage is this?" he said, "with you on one side of a wall, me on the other?"

"Oh, come off it," I said. "Couples do this sort of thing all the time. They live in separate apartments, on separate coasts, for god's sake. Our arrangement is hardly unique."

"I'm sick of it," he said. "I'm sick of sitting here and feeling like a failure. I'm done with it. I want out. Now!"

And then, before I could stop him, he started to struggle up through the glass bottleneck, his head in the canal, his feet kicking freely in the belly of the bottle, and I thought, "Oh god. Please no."

"Jack, don't!" I cried, but too late, the cork popped off and I could see his head inching over the thick glass lips, I could see his face all smushed in the canal, I could see how he curled up his feet and, placing them against the slick sides of his world, heaved himself into the air. He came out gasping and flopped onto the floor. He stood up, still miniature, and wiped his eyes on the cuff of his shirt.

"Fuck," he said.

And then he started to grow.

I started to cry.

"Damn bottle," he said at four feet. "Screw this shit," he said at about five-five. At six feet, his old height, he took his hand and swiped the bottle off the counter, so it smashed into a million pieces.

"You fool!" I cried. "You're out five minutes and already you're screwing up." I grabbed a broom and started to sweep the shards into a glinting pile. I swept up his rocking chair and tiny recliner, his miniature bed and that little hunk of ham.

"Throw it away," he said. His voice was deeper, more assured than I had ever heard it before. He held himself straight. For some reason my husband was now dressed like a matador. He had a red cape, a silk tunic top, vermilion stitching at his collar and cuffs. He wore ballooning pants tucked into hip-high boots, and he had a silver sword in his scabbard. The air crackled. He had changed. I was at once happy and horrified. I stared and stared at him. I saw myself tiny in his eyes.

The Fairy of Lost Things

THE SUMMER I turned ten, Mrs. Pichonio, the town widow, took in a stray girl. At first we thought the girl was a niece or a distant cousin here for a brief visit, but weeks passed and the girl didn't leave. We saw her at church with Mrs. Pichonio, and we saw her in the garden out back, among the huge red rhododendrons that surrounded the widow's house like a wall. That July and August were especially hot, cicadas everywhere in the humid nights, the moon always with an aureole around it. When fall came, cool winds cleared the air, and the girl stayed on, sometimes sleeping on Mrs. Pichonio's lawn. Everyone speculated. A rumor went around town that the girl had come from the other side of the mountains, her parents dead in a car crash. I myself believed the girl's parents had died in a house fire, because on her hand she had a burn that wouldn't heal. It glistened, always raw and pink like the skin lining a cheek.

To me, right from the beginning, the girl had an air of loneliness around her. She didn't seem to belong to anyone, including the old widow. The girl was in my class at school that year, and sometimes I saw her in the soccer field, kicking a stone. No one really talked to her, until the day Davy Rice went missing.

He was a twelve-year-old kid and one afternoon he didn't come home from his friend's house. Afternoon turned to evening, and Mrs. Rice grew frantic. A search committee formed, and all the men went out with flashlights, the beams crisscrossing in the dark air. Sometime around ten P.M., so the story goes, Mrs. Rice got a phone call, and it was from the girl, who simply said, "Look behind the dumpster at the skating rink," and then hung up. Mrs. Rice threw on her coat and hurried out to the rink, and sure enough, there was Davy, all crouched down. Not long after that Annie Crocker lost her cat, and the girl announced, "Hiding under the green Chevrolet on Mercy Street." In our house my mother had a statue made of white stone, a woman with wings, at the base an inscription: *The Fairy of Lost Things*. To me the girl was that swath of stone come to life.

Eventually, the mayor got wind of this girl who could bring back missing people, and he wanted to see for himself. He invited her to his offices. The mayor said, "Where is my wife, right this second?" And the girl said, "Aisle six, frozen foods, heading for the checkout." The mayor, in his black hat and serious suit, raced into town just as his wife was paying for the frozen vegetables, and word has it that he tipped his hat in a gesture of admiration. Word has it he walked slowly back to his office, and at some point, when the shock wore off, he started to smile.

OUR TOWN was essentially a safe town. We were surrounded by mountains few people ever crossed over, either to enter or to leave. We had a supermarket, a restaurant called Chat N' Chew, a soda fountain, a beauty parlor, and a clothing store that smelled like sawdust. Everyone knew everyone else. We'd always felt comfortable living here, but it's human nature to experience some unease. With the girl among us, though, her strange powers revealed, our mothers' fleeting worries evaporated. The year I turned ten we children were allowed to wander wherever we wanted. Dogs went without leashes; people even took down the sides of their outdoor playpens and let their babies crawl around corners. Our town grew almost festive. We had no milk cartons with pictures of missing children. My friends and I wandered to the edges of everything we could find; we started visiting a woman named Olivia, who had a tiny house right at the lip of the lake, where the ground was as soft as porridge. Olivia was beautiful. People said she had once lived in Paris, but she sought refuge here, in a simpler life.

Olivia always welcomed us in. She let us braid her straw-colored hair. We'd shriek, "Say nipple in French," and then fall over laughing. We were drawn to her because, I think, she knew another language, another way, and because she had a huge gilt-edged mirror and tiny bottles of scents that came from flowers and fields we knew we'd never get to.

For our freedom, the places we could get to, we had the girl to thank. But it wasn't long before we saw the unintended consequences of having her in our midst. While we were liberated we were also imprisoned. After a fight with your father, for instance, you couldn't hide out at a best friend's house until three in the morning, giving your folks such a scare they came to once again appreciate all your good points and your talents; high school kids couldn't stray way beyond curfew, even when they'd found that mossy spot in the woods. Wives couldn't say to a suspicious husband, "I'm going to the library," only to wind up in the bed of a policeman, because all that husband had to do was call on the girl. That advantage also applied to wives who wondered what really occurred when their husbands said they were working late. Not that it happened a lot, but sometimes, yes, we were human. The children had to say goodbye to certain sorts of secrets, the adults to others, and the town minister said this was a remarkable thing, to live where you couldn't get lost.

As I grew up, though, I started to want to get lost, just for the experience of it. I wanted to get so lost I was beyond reach of the human hand. How far, I wondered, did the girl's power extend? Could she find a person in Africa? Could she conjure up a dime lost in the distant deserts? I decided to do an experiment. I scraped some loose change off the hallway table, put on my explorer's cap, and left.

I didn't know where I was going. The sun was like a searchlight, high in the sky. I entered the woods that bordered the high school soccer field, and for a while I followed the paths beaten down by hundreds of boots and cleats, but then I veered off. I went left and right. I came, finally, to a steep hill, which I climbed, and found at the top a glossy ribbon of water. I followed that ribbon, letting it lead me far and farther away, until at last I arrived at a great lake, the water as smooth as Saran Wrap. In the middle, six black swans were swimming in circles. I watched those swans. The water was so clear I could see their pedaling feet.

Then the evening came. I knew I couldn't find my way home. I hadn't thought to drop bread crusts or cookie crumbs, something to mark my way. The sun turned the sky into a riot of reds. One by one the stars came out, some fuzzy and soft, others distant points of light. By now, I was sure, my parents had asked her to find me, and by now, I was sure, she was looking, peering under porches, parting the long milkweed that swayed at the edge of the swamp. Here, where I was, the black swans were beautiful; I clucked and one paddled over, gently pecked at my palm. The darkness thickened. The swans melted into it. The lake began to move, to mutter, its water creeping closer and closer with lewd sucking sounds. Far on the other shore, someone, or something, shrieked and shrieked at a depth of rage or sadness I had never heard before. When the moon appeared in the sky, I started to cry.

IT SHOULD COME as no surprise that the girl eventually located me, but not until nine o clock. "Your mother's really worried," she said. "You were supposed to be home for dinner." She held out her good hand and helped me up the hills, and I felt safe and smothered both.

She navigated us left and right, and not once did she trip on the rising roots of the trees, unlike me, who stumbled on almost all of them. At last, in the distance, I saw the twinkling lights of our town. I saw the black mountains rising behind it. I said, "You want to come over and play ping-pong sometime?" I was thinking about what the mothers sometimes said about the girl: She had no friends, poor thing; she had no extracurricular activities; she'd never get a chance to cheerlead. I thought of all I'd heard about the girl, so I invited her to play ping-pong. "No thanks," she said, as we exited the woods rimming the soccer field, beyond which was my school, beyond which was my house where I would always, always be brought back.

We faced each other. She was not a beautiful girl, but she had nice nut-brown hair and braces paid for by the mayor. "Would you ever, like, refuse to bring someone back?" I asked her. "Let's say it was someone you didn't like. Would you ever just say no if the parents asked you?"

Then the girl did something strange. She crossed her arms over her chest and hugged herself. She seemed to draw inward. That dreamy smile came to her lips, and her head cocked, like she was listening to a little silver bell far, far off. What could she hear? Maybe the sound of women on widows' walks, mourning for their sailors lost at sea? Or someone trapped underground, banging and banging on a pipe? She kept holding herself and rocking. "It feels good," she said at last, "to take me in my own hands."

WE PARTED soon after that. We stood still in that field, staring at each other, she holding herself in her own hands, until
at last she walked off across the soccer field, her hair float-
ing in the wind. "You go on home," she yelled over her
shoulder. "Your mother's made you lamb chops." And her
home? To whom did she really belong? People said they
sometimes saw her late late at night, wandering alone in the
widow's yard.

And now, as I watched her walking away from me, her
hair blowing, her wind-filled skirt almost holding her aloft,
it seemed to me she was a person who bore the weight of a
mysterious and awful freedom. She could go anywhere, at
any time. She could hide in a hole forever; she could travel to
Paris and back, or cross the mountains and step into the city,
where cars rumbled on busy roads and everywhere people
bustled, where there were tall buildings made of blue glass,
their tips touching the sky. At least that's what we heard. I'd
never seen it. But she had, or would or could, because no one,
nothing, seemed to keep a claim on her. And for a second I
felt it, the wideness of the world, how it just went on forever,

how terrible that was, and rich. I closed my eyes and pictured an ocean, a dolphin, the bottom of the sea where the fish had little lights. These were places she might go, whereas for me, I headed home. And sure enough, my mother had lamb chops in the warming drawer, and string beans. I knew exactly what would happen. I'd eat. Then I'd do my homework. Then I'd sleep. Then I'd go to school; then I'd go to college, for sure at Massasoit, the community college in town, because that's where everyone went. I had my life all laid out for me, like a sewing pattern where you could feel sure and safe in whatever it was you would make.

THE SPRING and summer of my tenth year passed in its own unremarkable way, and then the snow came and once or twice we saw the girl sleep in its mounds, leaving her shapes in the fresh fall. It was a long cold winter, one in which we didn't want to go outside, except to break off the fang of an icicle and suck it. When the spring came, the ground was soggy and we prepared to play, but something happened. There was a murder in our town. A murder! Olivia, the woman who lived in the tiny cottage at the lip of the lake, she'd been found stabbed to death on her living room floor, and people said the knife entered her heart so deeply it nicked the wood beneath. Citizens gleaned from the police that there were signs of a mighty struggle, the phone ripped from its cord, a couch overturned, an unmade bed, and on the comforter, a real rose. People shivered. The criminal had not been caught.

Now we started to lock up at night. Before turning off the lights, my father checked every window. Days went by and police were walking the streets, knocking on doors, asking for information. I saw a policeman knock on our neighbor Mrs. Jensen's door. It was evening then, and the windows in her home glowed like toffee. She came out onto the stoop, a head of lettuce in her hand, an apron around her waist, and I saw her shake her head no. I saw her shrug her shoulders. I saw her point to something, or someone, way down the dark road.

As the weeks went by and no one was apprehended, our town changed. Although no one said it, we were all considering each other as suspects. Who could ever really know what went on in the sealed space of a mind? Who could ever really comprehend his neighbor? This fact shook me up, how the mind is its own wide world, teeming with dreams, many beyond the reach of even our gifted girl. On the street, smiles became strained and the mountains surrounding us no longer seemed protective. The wind made sneering sounds in their peaks; animal eyes, yellow and hard, peered out from between the cliffs.

At last the police called in the girl. They hated to do it, because it didn't look good for their own abilities, but they did it. The police called in the girl and the town's newspaper reporter, Emily Doyle, wrote that they asked her to bring the murderer back from his hiding place. It was said the girl stood in the center of the police station, chewing on a hunk of hair. She stayed silent. Minutes went by.

At last she said, "I need a clue. Do you know his name?" No, they didn't. What he looked like? No, they didn't. Possible suspects? None. The girl then supposedly closed her eyes, like she was trying hard to summon up an image, but it wouldn't work. She started to sweat. She rocked back and forth on her heels. At last she said, "Try the belfry," and the police rushed to the church's belfry, where all they found were the feathers from pigeons and crows. Then she said, her voice growing anxious, "Try the ally behind the market," and all the police rushed there, waving their billy clubs, their gold buttons flashing. But no, nothing there except a cat. Then the girl started spewing out possibilities: the dressing room in the clothing store, Mr. Mandel's gardening shed, Billy Briant's treehouse; the more errors she made the more frantic she became, and the whole town gathered on the stone steps of the station to see the spectacle, the blue wave of police rolling out once more, and through the first-floor window, the face of the fallen girl.

AT LAST, after six or seven tries, she appeared on the stone steps of the police station, facing us, her palms held upward. "I need," she said, to the crowd, to the officers, "I need a face or a clue. I can't bring back someone who is unknown to me. All of you are known to me," she said, "and I appreciate it." Her voice started to tremble. "Please," she said, and then we saw her start to cry. *Please.* It was as if she were begging and apologizing at the same time.

The crowd murmured. We didn't know what to do. We hadn't until now come up against the limits of her powers. "Just try your best," someone shouted, and then Mrs. Levine walked right up the steps and put her arm around the girl, and the girl broke up into crying.

We all felt bad for the girl, of course, but more than that, we needed her help. We didn't love her. At school the next day, she hung her head and crossed her arms over her chest. We watched her.

Then the police got an idea. They decided to bring her to

the scene of the crime, where the blood was still fresh on the floor, where the ovoid nick of the knife could be seen in the wood. So they took her to Olivia's house, which was surrounded by yellow tape, and they brought her inside the crime scene. Who knew, maybe there was a strand of his hair left behind, or worse, a drop of his semen. Something to identify him, to make him marked.

Emily Doyle, the town newspaper reporter, wrote that the girl was brought into the wrecked house and that she saw bloody footprints, and the stained walls, and the kicked-in door, and the knick made by the knife. She supposedly started to shiver. She supposedly touched the place where Olivia had lain like she was remembering someone. Or something. One wrecked house. Now two wrecked houses. Someone screams. Fire! Fire! Her parents are gone! She stood still for a long long time, maybe thinking these things.

And then, all of a sudden, she snapped to—something must have been there, some smell, maybe—because she just snapped to and said, "He's hiding in the basement of the high school, behind the boiler, and he still has his knife, a bone handle."

And this time, she was right. The whole town rejoiced. The murderer turned out to be the school's janitor, whom no one really knew because, like Olivia, he was a recluse, and it comforted people, because in a very real sense he was not one of us; he was a stranger who did something strange. It made some sense.

We had a big festival in the park and all the grown-ups shook hands and the babies played and the kids wandered off freely to the Ferris wheel or even into the dark, but something was still wrong. We all felt a strain in the air. Who would have guessed? Who could have guessed? You couldn't for sure pin down the mind of anyone, maybe even yourself. Who would have thought the janitor? We understood then that the girl could bring things back, but there was a limit to our safety, a border, like the skin around our skulls, inside of which wrong things and right things were deeply hidden. We had had the experience of suspecting our own neighbors, if only for a fraction of a second, and that caused a kind of rupture. So even with the girl there among us and the man captured, parents kept a watch on their kids; kids like us went far but not too far, and when we rode the Ferris wheel we felt ourselves lifted, lifted, at last, to the top of the sky, where there were stars and darkness.

DURING that festival, the mayor made a speech. He said we could all return to normal now. He publicly gave the girl a prize, a cash-stuffed envelope and a piece of paper with a gold seal on it. The girl, who stood on the dais with the mayor, mumbled thank you thank you, and hung her head. And the very next day we awoke to cash drifting in the streets, bills in the drainpipes, bills caught in the tangle of a tree; her money was everywhere, but she was nowhere to be found.

She just disappeared from sight and we didn't know why. Mrs. Pichonio, her relative, didn't know why. She said that the girl's room was empty, but the bed where she sometimes slept retained the memory of her shape, her shadow, you could see it.

I think I know what happened. I think the girl was embarrassed by all the false leads she gave, by the clear evidence that her powers were limited, by the fact that she, who had created a net of security and safety—a net so tight it trapped and rocked us—had let us down, led us back to normal. I think she couldn't face us; she felt she was a fallen hero, and in a way it was true. She also knew she was unloved.

The day she left, we kids rushed outside to grab at the blowing bills. We bought Jujyfruits and cigarettes, maxi pads we put in the shoulders of our shirts, to give our plain clothes some stature. We bought dangly earrings, wore them, then lost them, along with car keys and soccer balls, library books and wedding rings, pet cats and cockatoos

which had taken to the trees. Of course, the people too—
every one of us—could also claim a secret hiding place again,
a place where a parent couldn't find you, or a cuckolded husband would never know to look. This made us both happy
and sad. As for me, a girl on the cusp of adulthood, a girl who
pictured a building of blue glass, a city teeming with trains
and cars, our tiny town suddenly seemed so paltry. The
mountains still surrounded us, their peaks sharp and black,
the trees there full of owls, whose wings you could hear in
the night, a waxy whisper.

I myself believe that the girl did go over the mountains.
For a while we talked about her, and then we talked less about
her, and then, by the time I was eighteen, we didn't talk about
her at all. I finished elementary school, and high school, and
sure enough, I went to Massasoit like everyone else, and I
took nursing, like all the other girls did, because there was a
hospital in our town, I think I forgot to mention that.

And of course, even though no one discussed the girl
anymore, I still thought about her a lot, how she had found
me at the silver lake, how she had led me home, which led me
here to here to here, how her hand felt enclosing mine. I
thought about watching those beautiful black swans and
then I thought about her, free in some distant city, where
opportunities were endless. She was a lion tamer. No, she

was a painter. No, she was a champion swimmer, with a bathing cap on her head.

Sometimes, I really had the urge to find her, but I knew I myself would never cross the mountains. Don't get me wrong. I loved my town even while I felt its belt around my belly. I got married. I had three kids and we all lived across the street from my in-laws. At night, my husband and I would touch beneath the blankets while our children slept, and then I would sleep, and often I would dream of her—or me—in a distant, unfamiliar place where a tawny lion roared and a ring of fire flared. Around me were tangles and tangles and tangles of streets, and huge houses with knockers in the shape of skulls and fists. There were women with high hair-dos and glittering buildings; it was me there, in the dream, and a stranger touched me, and when she finally found me, I felt so much relief. Whenever I awoke from that dream, it would be morning time already, the sun all orange, the sky the color of a creamsicle.

OTHER TIMES, though, the dream was different. Other times I actually dreamt I *was* the girl, and I had a great grief inside me. My burned hand hurt; it was impossible to hold; who would love me? Who would love her? I dreamt I was the girl walking through long tall grasses, and a river chuckled softly nearby, and the trees tented over me, and my life was loneliness and possibility warped into one. In these dreams, I walked and walked, over the mountains, across the streams, going here and there, going everywhere, until at last I came to a silver lake and then I was in a flaming house and I couldn't see; I couldn't see! They say you can't die in your dreams, but I did. I heard the screams of people around me. I felt my skin singe, and I struggled to stop it but it did no good. I was melting in a high heat. I relinquished everything. And then in this dream a liquid peace filled me as I crossed over, like her parents once had, like Olivia did, I crossed over to a place where black birds swam and the ground was covered with teeth. I went there, over the line, and as I did I knew nobody, not even she, could ever bring me back.

A Daughter's Tale

MY MOTHER, Queen Mei, lived in nineteenth-century Shanghai, where paper lanterns with star-shaped cutouts hung from all the trees, and in the night the stars were full of light, casting shadows on the street. My mother lived in the royal manor on the city's edge, among terraced gardens full of arum lilies, and tulips too, in certain seasons, wild tulips that grew along the garden's stony borders, with heads as bright as bubbles of blood.

My mother was elegant, like any royal woman must be. She had sculpted eyebrows, and lashes of black. Her skin was pale white on winter days, when the sky was stark, and on summer days it turned the color of a plum just as ripeness takes it from the tree, the fruit's flesh dark and glowing. She wore traditional royal garb, the emerald shantung silk, and, of course, her feet, pared back after years of careful smashing, always in their sweet white socks that hid the thickness of the bandages, a putrid smell she never let me near, a smell of black rot overlaid with heady and extravagant perfumes.

My mother was involved in very little, as far as daily life goes. My father ran the affairs, and my mother's job, especially before she had me, was to appear as Queen Mei, silent at his side, always smiling.

My mother had a little life and littler feet, but her memory was always capacious. Her past poured over her present, and she could tell the most amazing stories, but only when we were alone. She told me of the time before her feet were bound, when she was very young. Her family had lived, back then, in a northern region, where butterflies as big as books opened up on flowers. Before her own feet were bound she enjoyed some strange things—fishing, for instance, reeling from the water a hooked and crazed carp, which she would gut herself, this girl, slitting sideways with her brother's knife, her chest tight with excitement. She enjoyed her own body. She enjoyed especially the orchard that divided her family's estate from the neighbors', for in that orchard were all manner of things that a girl free on her feet could explore—lazy snakes and birds' eggs speckled with black. There were rocks to climb on and dirt to taste, and sometimes she imagined that the flowers were huge enough to crawl inside, which in her mind she did, scrunching her way back. Perhaps, I wonder, my mother knew what was coming, and wished she had not been born.

When she was six years old my mother's mother came to her to do her feet. The feet of a Chinese girl are bound slowly, over months, the rags and wrappings gradually tightened until the bones break and the stench must be masked with aggressive perfumes. My mother was playing outside when her mother and aunts called her in, telling her that now was the time, singing silly songs that did not mask the alarm in their eyes. *This old man, he played two, he played knick knack on my shoe;* that rhyme, and others, were sung to my mother as they did it, bending back the big toe, slowly folding the flexible foot with cinches. At first, lying in her room at night, my mother felt only tightness, but as time wore on a pain filled her lower limbs, and she cried out. Her own mother, weeping, said "Shhhush shush, my girl." I imagine my own mother lying there in the dark while her bones dissolved and the fibers flexed backward, and she must have thought of shaping topiaries, how the gardeners took the huge knives and scalpeled off growths, bent fibrous twigs to achieve, against all odds, a snake, or a great green box.

———

"FLOWER, FLOWER," my father called my mother. He was a man with black hair, and he loved my mother like one might love a toy. "My little flower," he said, and handed her gifts and once a green parrot in a bamboo cage. As for himself, he was busy running the province.

Three months into their marriage, my mother got pregnant. This surprised her, that her body could carry a ripe egg, because she herself was so frail. She told me she prayed and prayed that the little egg would become a boy, but it didn't. It became me.

Like my mother, I have a vast, untethered memory, a memory that cannot be bound. Therefore it is in all truth that I tell you how well I recall my conception, the night (it was rainy), the way he rode her, hard and bucking, joyful and selfish, his buttocks way up, her hand like a small starfish clasping them, a clasp not in passion but in pain. Why, if this is so, do I find a little ripple of desire in me when I tell this part of the tale? My mother's little hand. His large and flaring buttocks. The tiny doll-sized feet. His mouth with all their teeth. Why does a cord tighten in me, a tiny catch in my breath? I cannot stand it.

I remember the way it rained, the clouds scudding across the sky, the spurt of sperm, the warm reddish walls of the world I grew in. I remember my feet forming, each bone a white wire that gradually hardened, here a heel, now toes, how beautiful are the toes, turning the foot into a candelabra. I remember kicking my feet and feeling the rubbery give of my mother's womb, and I loved her then, immediately. I also remember turning my eye upward, looking straight up the shaft of her body, to her mouth where a prick of light entered, and hearing her say, "I pray for a boy, because I could not bear to love a girl." I loved her just naturally, without ambivalence, but already, right from the first fleck of my being, she loved me with taint and hesitancy. Sometimes I see it that way. Other times I see that she loved me with so much passion she was left with no choice but to want to protect me, and protection meant erasure. I was not wanted and then again, I was.

I was born breech. The first thing my mother saw of me were my feet. They dangled from her body, and the attending pulled me out, and I got stuck. For a few bad minutes my head was stuck in my mother's lower extremities, the rest of my body swinging free. "Push," the attending screamed, while I struggled for air, and I was born feet first, kicking, wild, very alive but blue.

She fondled my feet. This would become a habit of hers that I detested, but, at first, I did not know enough to detest. Newly born, still streaming with water, she reached down and fondled my tiny perfect feet, and she put them in her mouth, which she should not have done. She counted I had ten toes. She pressed in at the tender heel. She fell in love with my feet and from there moved upward, falling in love next with my knees, my nipples, at last my face.

My mother cried when I was born. She cried when she suckled my feet. For hours afterward she held the trinket that was my body and thought of what my life would be like, I with maybe five free years and then the bone-breaking pain, a life of hobble. Her heart was sodden and also exuberant, for I was something, I know I was, my eyes open and unfocused, my hand moving across the sheet, my mouth bearing down on her engorged nipple with such a fierce claiming suck. On the one hand, she could not imagine that there might be an adult hidden somewhere in my tiny pupal body; on the other hand, she saw my nipples and vagina, swollen from being in her body, bright dribbles of blood. "Oh, it will go away, its what girl babies do," said the attending, but the blood, it was menstrual, dark and blackish on her hand, and in it she smelled my sex and time.

I hate that my mother smelled my sex and time. I love that she watched me with devotion, and that I, opening my eyes to a room stung with bright light, saw first her face and then her enlarged breasts, which were so good and planetary. She was a world.

I grew up like my mother did in her own early years. I ran and played on my free feet. I thought of my birth often. I also thought of lizards and training a turtle to talk. I was childish. I had a strange streak of black hair that ran from my ribs to my pudendum, a stripe of silk that grew in when I was two and darkened, and was very odd. Some people said that I was not a child at all, but an evil spirit. Some people of the district said I had crooked powers, and claimed they had witnessed me walking backward through doorways. I was two, I was three, I was a royal girl. My father, horrified, avoided me. This, of course, made me only love him more. I'd trail along after him like a pathetic little animal and offer to get him things, his slippers, his beard cutter. He would shoo me away. When I clambered after him for affection, his body would stiffen, and the stiffness set off a huge hunger in me. At night I fingered the silky stripe of my hair, letting my hand trail lightly from its start at my ribs to the peak of the pudendum, but I never went any lower than that. I touched around and around, and felt a great unresolved excitement arise in me.

Age five or six is the time when a mother and her aunts

usually begin the binding process. I turned five, and then six, and then seven, and my mother did not approach me. I ran on bare feet. My hair was straight and dark and hung to my hips. My father said, "You must bind the girl now," he said this to my mother, calling her "you," or "little lotus," but, increasingly as the years went on, just "you."

And still, my mother would not bind me. Several times, at night, she came to my room with the white wrappings and a bowl of steaming water, and she would sit at the foot of my bed and cry, and her sadness was my sadness, and I said, "It's okay, Mama," but I didn't know what I was saying. I only wanted her to stop crying. I only wanted my father to love me. I only wanted my mother to not look at the way I ran with such a longing and a fierceness in her eyes. She touched my feet. I felt devoured by devotion, unseen and too seen, and meanwhile, I grew, and the black stripe of hair that ran from my ribs migrated like a coat, incomplete wisps here and there, under my arms, on my legs, wiry hair like the bristles from a paintbrush, they sprung on my upper lip, a dark down, as though I really were a boy, and that made me wish for nothing more than to be a girl.

I watched the other girls in my school closely. They were pink and pretty as frosting. One by one, they became dear and diminutive. One by one their feet turned into ladies' feet, fit for slippers and the pure white socks. Only I, my mother's child, the embodiment of all her wishes, only I stayed large and lumbering. Only I could run in the pastures, only I could climb a tree, and, as I grew, there were fewer and fewer girls to do this with me.

"Play with the boys," my mother said, my mother whispered to me late at night, and I hated her then, for I was not a boy, was I? But then again, maybe I was; I looked at the little girls, and their little feet, and I was shot through with desire, but what sort of desire was it? Did I desire to be those girls, or to touch them? I was twelve, and very confused.

My mother and I bathed together sometimes. I don't think I have conveyed how close we were, as angry as I sometimes was. And, as I got older, we grew perhaps closer still, for I had fewer and fewer friends, and my father slunk from my touch. We bathed together in a private creek that ran outside the castle, and she washed my back with moss and we pulled earthworms, their segmented centers bulging, from beneath stones. She came to the meadows with me, and when no one could see, screamed, "Run, little one, run," and she cheered as I spun and ran and then we lay back, and chewed on grass. My mother came alive with me as she never did at home, as she never did around my father or the servant women, and I felt so happy to give her the gift of aliveness, and sometimes, at night, she came to my bed and we lay close.

Then, one day, my menses came. This was to be expected, of course. My father said, "If you do not bind her feet now, you, my wife, will be committing a major crime, a crime against the province and its laws."

My mother nodded. She took me to a chamber and showed me how to swab the blood. Word got out that I was bleeding. This was the time when the rumors intensified. Word got out that I was seen leaving plates of food for restless evil ancestors, who inhabited my body. Word got out that I had a tail, that a horn grew on my hip, and that I had kissed a schoolgirl on the stomach. Many thought I was a piece of warped energy that flew as a fragment from an angry god, nestled in my mother's womb, and grew there. The attending who had delivered me said, "I do remember, she came feet first," and everyone murmured, as though this were evidence. At school I followed the girls, and while most of the rumors were not true, it is true that I did kiss one girl on the stomach. Sometimes girls took me home with them, and then I got to see the special rooms where they went all by themselves to unwrap their wrappings. I was never allowed into those rooms. I kissed a girl on the stomach—

her name was Layla—and she laughed and took me home with her, and then she shut me outside while she changed, while servants brought her steaming bowls of liquids, flowers floating on the top. "Layla, Layla," I called from outside the door, "can I come in, please, can I see you and your feet?" But she said, "No, this is woman's work and you are not a woman." The servants brushed past me. Because I was outside the door, I could not smell the stink of Layla; I could only smell the heady scents of jasmine, and I could only imagine how she lifted her skirts, her bare white knee.

When Layla came out, she smiled at me, a supercilious, beautiful smile. No one was in the hall then; the servants disappeared. She reached out and touched the dark down on my upper lip. I did not understand the rising inside me. I did not understand if I wanted to touch Layla or be Layla. I dreamt of her. I kissed her again one day, like a girl, like a woman, like a man, and this time she pulled away. "Devil," she hissed. She wiped her mouth with the back of her hand. She tottered off snickering with the other girls and would not speak to me again.

That night, my mother came to my room, as she often did, her face increasingly drawn and worried, for if she did not bind me, she would be committing a crime of the highest offense. "Do you see that wall over there?" she said to me, pointing out my darkened window to a high stone wall that separated our wealthy province from the land beyond it.

"Yes," I said.

"Beyond that stone wall live the peasants. They spend their days gathering vegetables and fruits, and at night they dance, and they live their lives always with their feet unbound and free."

I thought of Layla; I thought of the pretty petite other girls. I thought of my father's disgust toward me, and wanted this remediated. "I am not a peasant!" I said to my mother. "I am your child, your girl, born into this family."

"If you escaped over that wall," my mother said to me, "you could live with your real legs always."

"You want me to go," I said. I started to cry.

"No, no," she said, "I want you to live."

"I am not alive," I said. I cried and I cried then. "I am different and dark and I will not be alive until you treat me like the others, until you bind up my feet."

My mother pushed me away, looked at me. "You want me to bind your feet?" she said. "All these years I have been working and risking my life to protect your feet, and you would feel better if they were bound?" She snorted. I had never seen my demure mother angry before. I had certainly never seen her snort. "Do you know what you are talking about?" she said. "Do you know what life will be like for you? Do you know you will never take one solid step again, that you will be the sexual slave of a man who cares only for your stumped appendages, that you will have no dignity, that twice a week you will have to bathe your warped walking things, prying apart the gelatinous dead flesh"—and here she was screaming—"and then smearing it over with perfume?"

She was screaming, but I could not hear her. I could only think of being on the outside of the girls' doors, on the outside of the girls' world, my hair too dark and spiky. I thought my mother hugely selfish, for it was she who wished for free feet, not me. I wished only to be like Layla, or to touch Layla, the distinction did not matter.

"Go," I said.

"All right," my mother said. "You want what you want. We will do it, then. Tomorrow at midnight, come to my room. Come in a white dress, with a white cloth, and we will begin."

THE NEXT NIGHT the moon was large and red. I ran down to the creek and lay in the shallow water. It was not yet dark, despite the full-bodied moon. I watched my pelt lift and sway in the current. I watched my feet, far at the other end of me, break through the silvery skin of the liquid, whole and strong, but not for long. "Goodbye feet," I said. Did I feel sad? I called on my memories. I called on the time when my feet were first formed, tiny and exuberant, pedaling fast in the water-world. I examined the feet of a slithery salamander that lay on a rock near me, its tiny clawed toes and bones too petite to be possible, and in a branch above me the trefoil feet of a black bird, and the rooted toes of trees branching out across the ground, and it suddenly seemed the world was all about feet, motion as essential as breath, but then the thought passed. The salamander slipped into the water. The bird flew away. I rose, put on a formal white gown, and walked to my mother's room.

I SHOULD have known. Her room? The bedroom? Foot bindings never take place in those kinds of quarters; they happen in special chambers at the west wing of a home. The bedroom my mother directed me to was not west, but north. I should have known. I was happy with anticipation but numb with fear. The stone corridor smelled of silt and candle wax and in the caverns were the candles, droplets of luxurious wax beading their slender sides. The candles sputtered; the wicks crisped; outside, the cranes streaked into the sky. The corridor was long and twisty. The door to the bedroom was only half closed. From its innards came the delicious and cloying odors of petals soaked in oils, and heavy sweat. I heard churning and urgent whisperings. I heard it before I saw it. I felt it before I saw it. What I felt, a little peak, a hot point of flame in the lowest part of my belly. Something about those sounds, the silky slitherings. I pushed open the door and stood there.

They were on their massive bed, my mother and father. I saw my father's opium pipe, an intricately curled thing, and his heavy drunken movements made it obvious he had smoked quite a bit that night. He was mounting my mother, so he could not see me, and would not have seen me anyway, even if he had looked right at me, for I was never visible in his eyes. As for her, her weak white legs were spread, and he was on top of her, he so big, she so small, her diminutive feet wrapped in special erotic socks, pink as a cat's mouth, those special socks, and he reached down, grabbed her ankle, said, "Oh, my little, oh, little little." He pawed at her feet, his buttocks thrusting high and tan, a little nick in the skin just where the spine stopped, and he was speaking all clotted, "So little," he was saying, and then he must have been inside her,

"So slippery," he moaned, "too slippery and small to ever get away from me, all mine, all mine," and then, all of a sudden, he stopped. He stopped moving.

"Say, 'I am so small,' " he said to my mother, still on top of her.

"I am so small," I heard her say, her voice flat and clicking.

"Say, 'I will never get away.' "

She was silent. The silence lasted for maybe a second, but a second is not so small; in between the brackets that shape a second things of austere beauty and grave horror can happen; a fruit hits its precise point of ripeness, and falls perfect from a tree, only later to blacken with flies.

My mother moved her head. He grabbed her hair and said, "Say it." She looked over his shoulder and saw me standing there, just as she had planned it. She had said, "Come for the binding," so she could show me what a binding really was. My mother and I stared at each other, she under him, me at the threshold of the room. Our eyes met, mine fierce with hunger and disgust, hers flat and dead, as if to say, "So now you see," and then she announced, to both of us, of course, "I will never get away," and he pushed deeper in.

I RAN, THEN. I ran out of the castle and into the farthest garden, where, on the other side of the wall, the peasants lived
and worked. I lay on the dirt and smelled it, all the bodies of
the earth, it was too much. She had wanted to thwart me, to
teach me a lesson, but all it did was burn me with a desire
too twisted to be true, but it was true! How deliciously small
she was. The pleasure of erasure. The rising of buttocks and
the blackness of his hair, my hair, I had a pelt. I had a stripe
of soft down on my upper lip. I had the two tiniest breasts,
soft enough for me to squeeze, and yet my feet were hard and
large. I loved it all. I slipped my hand beneath my gown and
stroked myself, and when it happened, when the point rose
so high it tipped, I felt not pleasure but rage.

Then I got up, hating myself. The truth is, watching my
parents, I had wanted to be my father and hold my mother,
my back broad and royal and flanked with muscle, say it. You
will never get away. The perversion of love. The duality in a
single skin. Say it. I kissed a girl and was a girl. Both these
things were true.

The night had matured now, the darkness full. I stood up
and walked slowly down the path and into our province's
center. People bustled about, cutting wide swaths around me,
because I was the king's daughter, and also cursed. I started

to cry. I went to the seamstress, whom I knew for her excellent shawls and lace work. She was still at work, sewing by the light of a thick candle, wax pooled around its erect wick. "What is wrong?" she said to me, and I said, "My mother, my mother has betrayed my father. She does evil acts with peasant women. She brings the bones of Lie [a dragon known to be evil] into our home, and uses them to—" I stopped.

"To what?" the seamstress said.

I pointed to my pelvis. I made a lewd motion with my hand. The seamstress backed away. I slept outside that night, underneath a pear tree.

IT DID NOT take long. Word got to my father about his queen's infidelities, with women, no less, and she was arrested. My father said, "Now I know why she would not bind the poor girl's feet, why the girl was born with a hide of hair. A curse has been upon us."

My mother was taken away to a jail. Her hands were bound with white cloth, so she lost those too, and from the city's center I could hear her as they worked on her, and her cries were unendurable; I covered my ears. And when they finally let her out she had admitted it all; she was broken, weak, with no teeth, she said yes to conjuring the bones of

Lie and using them for fornication, to bedding with women while she was pregnant with me, thus causing a coat of darkness to mantle my body. She said yes, she had refused to bind my feet in the hopes of shaming our province. They hung her on a Sunday. A crowd gathered and pressed. She climbed upon the platform, and just before she fell, her gaze caught mine and I wanted nothing more than to have her chest on mine. Mother.

The crowd quieted. She stood on the platform. "Run," she said. I ran. I ran past the terraced gardens and the creek where we used sponges of moss and Layla's house; I ran to the wall and climbed over it, and fell to where the peasants were, standing on their free and dirty feet.

THIS WAS ALL a long, long time ago, in another world. I am a grown person now, past the age of tumult and terrible passion. There are gods you can pray to for forgiveness, but I do not, because you must be human to pray, and I am something altogether less. I lived on the other side of the wall, going from village to village, my clothes getting torn, picking fruits with the peasants, and selling them, or eating them raw and fly-infested, and I grew up. The hairs darkened and filled in. I have my father's broad shoulders, but I think I have my mother's feet, what they would have been, had they been able to grow, slender like boats, packed with motion and muscle, they take me everywhere, but everywhere I go, I am sad.

After a while, maybe when I was seventeen, maybe when I was eighteen, I stopped looking like a girl, because I stopped trying to look like a girl, and so I looked like a boy, with my lip of hair and thick eyebrows. Some of the peasant women thought me handsome, and many wanted me. I wanted them. I dressed like a man and walked like a man. I kissed women like a man, but that was all, because nakedness would show I was not a man; I was a woman with a heart so large and violent it bucked blue in my chest. I have never understood myself. I have certainly never forgiven myself. Sometimes, when I kiss a woman, I think of my mother, and how, when I was born, she held me up beneath my tiny armpits, swung me in the air, and let me latch onto her breast, where my mouth has maybe never left. I think of that sometimes and feel desire rise up in me. Other times though, when I kiss a woman, I think of my father's broad back, the strength and ugliness with which he rode her, and desire again rises up in me, fans out across my own broad back. All I know for sure is this. I wander from village to village. At night I dream of many things. I dream of cherries. I dream of bats. I dream I kiss a girl and then cannot stop. I grab her hair, bind her feet—she is so small! So sweet!—I cannot stop; I bind her up the legs, the belly, the breasts, the neck, and then I unwrap her to touch, but the bandages are covering only air now, and I see the girl is gone.

No No No

THERE WAS a young woman who lived alone where many seals swam. Her house was at the icy edge of a sea. The seals swam in the sea and the young woman watched the seals, because she had no other company.

The young woman had no other company because she was ugly. Her left leg was longer than her right, and she badly limped.

Perhaps because she was ugly, the young woman wanted nothing more than to be beautiful. She had dreams in which she was beautiful, with graceful fingers and feet.

And then one winter morning many men came to the sea and clubbed the seals to death and took all the bodies away, except for one, a small one. The young woman was bereft, and then, on the third day of her bereavement, she went outside her house and found the small dead seal in the snow, and slit it open. Out came the heart, and the beautiful bones, which were flexible as wet reeds and whistled like flutes when the wind got to them, but the woman did not want the bones. She did not want the heart or the spongy lungs. She wanted the skin, for there is nothing in the world quite like sealskin, at once oily and soft; she put it on.

Wearing the sealskin, the young woman slipped into the sea and felt fully warm and free. She moved in the ocean like she never could on land, and when she dove under, she had no need for breath, her flippers moving her fast past the jungly underworld where all was green and wavy. Her own heart lifted then, and at the same time, although she had no way of knowing, the red heart scooped out on the snow began to beat, and then turned into a cardinal and flew away.

The woman, in the sealskin, swam past a village where many people lived and shopped. She swam so fast and held her nose so high and proud above the water that everyone stopped to admire her. And the woman, who had never been admired before, got bold before the villagers. She turned in circles and did a flip. She stood tall on her tail and shimmied. The villagers threw ribbons and clapped. When at last darkness came and the clapping went away, the woman missed the sound and so, the next day, she went back for more. Day after day she danced for the villagers, leaping and diving and turning in circles, and the more they watched her, the harder she worked. She grew tired, but she could not stop. And then she grew very tired, but she could not stop. At night, float-ing alone in the waves, the woman realized she had once liked her loneliness.

And then winter arrived again, and again the men came back and clubbed a new crop of seals to death. They clubbed the woman to death too, because they thought she was a seal, but when they opened the animal up and inside found a woman, they were horrified. Standing in the snow-draped woods, the hunters lifted her body and wept. They cradled her in their arms. They fed her hot broth from a thermos. They smoothed back her hair, and because they loved her like a human, she opened her eyes.

And for some reason now, the young woman was beauti-ful. The broth brought a flush to her cheeks. She had glossy black hair and glossy black eyes, plus both her legs were strong.

The hunters saw the girl with her eyes open; they saw the supple way she yawned and stretched. They gasped and murmured, just like the villagers had when they saw her as a seal. Only now the young woman was wiser. She knew about performance, and she also knew the quiet nights alone, floating in the water.

However, the hunters understood none of this. They only

knew they wanted to marry the young woman so they could gaze upon her all of their days. The first hunter proposed to her, promising her a house with a purple roof, to which she said no. The second hunter promised her a horse with a mane of real silver, to which she said no. The third hunter said, "If you marry me, I vow to give you a garden in which the roses yield honey even in the winter," and to that she also said no. The fourth hunter spoke slowly. He said, "Marry me, my dear, and every time we kiss a coin will fall from our lips, and we will grow rich and happy."

And to that the girl said—

"No."

No no no she said to all of their proposals. All she could think of was the sound of their clubs coming down, the slice of their knives, and before that, spinning in circles, which is why she said no to the hunters.

And she grew ever more beautiful with each refusal, her hair growing glossier, her eyes like onyx, her limbs so strong!

"Goodbye," she said to the hunters who had killed her but also somehow strangely brought her back to life, and then she simply left them. She went away, out of the woods and down the lane, back to her own house at the icy edge of the sea, where she spent her days growing cucumbers. And then, much later in life, she married a blind man; he didn't know night or day or the specific shape terror might take; his world was all touch and his eyes were such that he could stare straight into the sun. And she loved him. And sometimes with his fingers he felt her face; he felt around her eyes, and her mouth; he felt the bones in her back and the throb at her neck; he felt her shiny scars and the flatness of her feet. Sometimes he stood back and stared straight at her, and she knew she was seen.

Fur

ABOUT ONE week after my twelfth birthday I found, in my parents' dressing room, certificates revealing that they were born hundreds of years ago, my mother in 1745, my father in 1743. Their dressing room was small and cluttered, with a bank of brown drawers from which, I now noticed, small moths were flying. On a green strip of velvet, my mother's earrings twinkled. My father's slippers, when I slid my hands inside them, were warm and full of twigs. Crouching there, I began to understand my parents in a new way—why they never fit into our town; why they avoided the yearly carnival with its mechanized rides and bumper cars; why they refused to fly in planes. I understood their terrible taste in clothes, my father in his big bowler hats, my mother's hatred of short skirts, her love of riding sidesaddle, her handmade things.

I had always been embarrassed by my parents, and at the

same time, I had always loved them like one might love an odd-looking animal, something mangy and smart and sweet. I was only twelve, but out in the world it was I who instructed them—here is the *right* gift to get; don't wear *that* to the dinner party—while at home they instructed me. My mother taught me how to make a one-eyed Egyptian for breakfast, cutting a circle out of hot, home-baked bread, frying a yolk in its center. My father spent hours teaching me to fence. Afterward, his hand on my head, my head on his solid shoulder.

And now, these certificates. The dressing room where I stood had a tiny porthole window through which late afternoon sun flamed and streamed. And I felt then, as I folded back the papers, a kind of horror and hilarity all at once. I covered my mouth with my hand.

That night, after I climbed into my bed, my mother came to me. She always stroked my hair, scalp to tip, as I fell asleep. "Mummy," I said. I said it very softly. She didn't hear. In the shadows, her face looked smudged, her eyes at once sunken and flat. She was so much older than I'd ever noticed before. I saw for sure how she would die someday. *Soon soon,* the air seemed to whisper.

I felt my bones.

I fell asleep.

When I awoke the next day, I noticed my mother had a little whisker growing out of her mole. I went to school, worried. My teacher told me to stop staring out the window. At home in the evening, my father, usually spry, complained about a body part called the coccyx.

My mother, looking wan, touched her nose with her finger. "I smell something funny," she said. "Sarah," she said to me, "do you have on perfume?"

Truth was, I did, a little bit of perfume that I'd filched from the pharmacy, in a small bottle with a heart-shaped top. Just moments before I had stood in the bathroom, by the mirror, dabbing it here and there on my pulse points, my underarms, my chest, which was softening and tender to the touch.

HERE'S WHAT happened. I started to see both my parents slow down. At first I thought I was looking for it, but no, objectively speaking, they were getting sick. Especially my mother. Her face was pale, the skin on her hands spotted with browns and purples. She couldn't climb our front stairs without gasping. "She's dying," I thought. I thought of her hand on my hair at night. I thought of how he held me, the smells of their skins, of comfort. All that was going. I thought about how someday I would turn seventeen, and for some reason that word, *seventeen*, it sounded so sharp and lonely.

Then it was a Saturday. She was retching. I went into the kitchen. "You need to see a doctor," I said. "You know," I said, my voice rising, "a *doctor*. What we in our day and age call an *M.D.*"

"I know what an M.D. is," my mother said.

"Sarah, you have a rude tone to your voice," my father said. He was sitting at the table, drinking coffee from a chipped cup.

"I appreciate your concern," my mother said. "It's just a flu."

"How old are both of you?" I said then. My father looked up quickly and exchanged a sharp, meaningful glance with my mother. "Forty-one," my mother said. "Forty-five for me," my father said, and a moth flew out of his hair.

"Liars, liars," I whispered inside myself.

ON SUNDAY, the doorbell rang, and on the welcome mat stood our family practitioner, Doc Giverson, in a white coat, carrying a test tube full of blood.

"May I come in?" he said.

My parents ushered him inside. We all stood in the hall.

Doc Giverson gave my mother a wink. "Everything's fine here," he said, handing her the tube of blood. "Electrolytes, cholesterol, liver function. Thing is," he said, "you're pregnant."

My mother's eyes widened and she put a hand to her stomach.

"At my age?" she said.

"Think young, stay young," Doc Giverson said. "That's my philosophy."

I looked from my father to my mother, and back again.

"You're not going to *have it*?" I said.

My mother rubbed the bridge of her nose.

"It's not an *it*," she said. "It's a he. Or a she." My mother smiled.

"Still a stallion!" my father shouted.

"Daddy," I said. I turned away.

It was then that I began to eat. I couldn't seem to help myself. I ate candied dots on strips of long white paper, Jujyfruits, and mayonnaise straight from the jar, scooping it up with my hands. I read diet books, the Atkins Diet, the Hollywood Grapefruit Diet, but those books only made me hungrier. McDonald's french fries, and wedges of dark cake drizzled with whitish icing. My arms plumped out, my cheeks got pudgy; even my toes took on some weight, but I still looked like a little girl, which was good.

My MOTHER, on the other hand, my ancient, antique, aging mother, she grew and grew and looked nothing like a little girl. She seemed to delight in her state, even though it made her tired. One afternoon, my mother and I stood together in the laundry room, in the basement of our house. The ground-level windows let in the late afternoon sun, a bright blaze that turned the trees to torches. My mother was hand-washing a linen blouse, the lather too rich for my taste, tiny seeded bubbles hatching in her hands.

The doctor suggested, given her age, that she have ultra-sounds, which she refused. Her belly expanded to such a size that she needed help rolling over and standing up. My father just got prouder. "Stallion," he kept saying, like I didn't exist, because that's not what you say in the presence of your child. I was a child, wasn't I? How old was I, really? I was grow-ing fuzz under my arms. I kept my arms clenched close to me, so no one could see.

"Aren't you guys too old to have a baby?" I kept saying.

"Don't you want a sister or a brother?" my father said, drawing me close, nicking my cheek with his chin, which is the best chin in the world, my father's, always stubbly and soft at the same time. I started to cry.

"Don't you want to not be a one and only anymore?" my mother said, putting her heavy arm around me. "What's wrong, Sarah?"

"I don't want to ever turn seventeen!" I said. My parents looked confused.

"Would sixteen be okay?" said my father. I couldn't answer. I couldn't explain. Seventeen scared me because of the magazine. In it there were always girls with velvet chokers on their necks, like something slashed there. Or there were girls in tiny swimsuits, in the ink-blue ocean, where the sharks swam.

On July Fourth, we were eating lunch on our porch, and my mother went into labor. "Ooops," she said, putting down her ham sandwich. I heard something splash, and then the indoor/outdoor carpeting was soaked. We all rushed to the hospital, in a taxi, of course, because neither of my parents knew how to drive. My mother was panting in the backseat. The cabdriver looked anxious. "Go go go," he said, when my father fumbled in his pants pocket for the fare. "Just go!" he said as we idled by the ER doors, and then he sped off, unpaid, his tires like a screech of relief.

Inside the hospital, my mother climbed onto a bed. She

refused any painkillers, saying, "Women did without for centuries, you know." It was terrible to see my mother in such
agony. She twisted and crouched. She shifted positions, the
worst one being, as far as I was concerned, the belly-on-the
bed-butt-in-the-air formation. My father was on a high. He
kept dashing into the waiting room and offering people
cigars, before the baby was even born. Sometime around
midnight, my mother started to cry, sounds I never knew
could come from a woman's mouth. They were man-sounds,
thick and guttural. "Mom, mom," I kept whispering.

At last it was time to push. Now a doctor came in
through the doors and said, "Push!" and she pushed. Her
belly was moving and rolling. Night edged into early morning. My mother screamed. Through the hospital window I
saw the moon, and it scared me. It was a full moon,
absolutely round, like a huge lost polka dot in the sky.

"Here comes the head," the doctor finally said. I stood
way out of the way, by my mother's shoulder, my fingers in
her hair. My father stood by my mother's legs, with the doctor. "Here it comes," my father shouted, and then, and then,
it got very quiet.

"Oh my," at last someone said, a nurse, I think.

"Is everything okay down there?" my mother asked, sitting up on her elbows, trying to get a glimpse of herself where it's not easy to see.

"Oh my," said someone else.

I couldn't help myself then. I went to look. Between her splayed legs was a head, but it was not a baby's head; it was the head of a very old old man, wearing spectacles. He coughed into his fist and shimmied himself the rest of the way out, his legs last; he back-flipped off the bed and landed flat on his feet on the floor.

The old man stood then, looking around him, flicking bits of goop from his suit. "For god's sake, people," he muttered. He was bearded, like a creature from a fairy tale, maybe Rumpelstiltzkin. "For god's sake," he said again, and, tipping his head sideways, tried to knock some water out of his ear. We were all so silent. The old man looked from my father to my mother to me. He blinked his eyes, dabbed them dry with a hospital blanket, and then leaned over to inspect some machinery.

"Who are you?" my father said.

My mother looked crestfallen.

The doctor went to wrap the newborn in some swaddling, which really irritated him. He was already dressed, after all, in some kind of suit, with a gold chain and a pocket watch.

"Morris?" my mother said, squinting, leaning forward. "Are you Morris?" That was her brother, who died five years ago from lung cancer.

"Not Morris," he said. He honked into his handkerchief.

"Erasmus?" said my father, leaning forward, grasping him by the shoulder. I had no idea who Erasmus was. "Are you Erasmus?" he said.

"Nope," the old man said. He said it with a little snicker.

"Rumpelstiltzkin," I said.

The little old man laughed with glee and hopped on one foot, so I was sure I was right, but then he said, "Nope. Charles Darwin, come back to test some theories."

My mother, flopping back in the pile of pillows, snorted. The doctor backed out of the room. My mother said, "Oh, come off it. The least you can do is tell us the truth."

"Yeah!" I said, and the old man looked at me so severely, I stared at the floor.

"Josiah!" my father said, a smile breaking out onto his face. "You must be my nephew Josiah, died of scarlet fever—"

"Darwin," the old man said, and, pulling a monocle from his pocket, peered at a geranium plant on the windowsill.

"This is bad enough," said my mother, her voice quavering, "this is . . . shocking enough that the least you can do is be straightforward about your identity," and then she broke into sobs, could not speak.

DESPITE his protestations, the doctors came back in and put so-called Charles under the drying lights—he was wet, after all—and then settled a small knit cap on his head. I myself didn't know what to make of Charles. Mostly, I couldn't even think about him. I felt so sad for my mother. She cried and cried. My father stood by her bedside, stroking her shoulder. "Hey, it's a beautiful thing, Margaret Ann," he said to her, "birth is always a beautiful thing," and she said, "All that for some schizophrenic old man?"

Nevertheless, this man was ours. The next day, stoically, my mother wrapped him up and we carried him home from the hospital. We put him in the guest room. It did not take long for him to make the room his. Maps of strange lands and sketches of lizards appeared on the walls. Specimen jars lined the shelves, each one filled with dried insects or curled leaves of plants. I awoke one night, very late, to a strange sound outside my bedroom window. He was on our lawn, the moon bathing him in light. He was on all fours, digging in the dirt, pulling up worms, which he seemed to study, and then making notes on loose pieces of paper. I tapped on the glass. He looked up, beckoned me out. Out I went. The grass was wet on my bare feet. The earth seemed spongy beneath me. I wanted to ask him about age, what was possible if you traveled through time, if he could explain to me my parents, and somehow, by extension, myself. The eighteenth century. The twenty-first century. Growing old and starting to smell.

I had questions, but no words.

I stood facing him, the night air dense. Crickets creaked in the grass. "Without insects," he said, "our entire planet would collapse." He put a worm in my hand. It was lipstick-pink, and sticky. It curled into a coil and I shook it from my palm. I had a hundred questions, but instead all I said was, "You're not my brother." Charles looked at me for a long time. A bird flew by. He said, "Kinship extends farther than you can imagine. Even the worms are your brothers."

The next morning, all three of us, me, my father, and my mother, trudged into the guest room to bring Charles his breakfast, as we did every morning, a bottle of milk and tamarind biscuits. However, something must have happened, because he was no longer there. The bed was empty. My mother, whom I suddenly realized had been coming, slowly, to love the old guy, clapped her hand over her mouth. I had never seen such sorrow in her before, and it filled me with sorrow too. I remembered how I'd said, "You're not my brother," and then I felt guilt.

I knew what to do. Somehow this knowledge just came over me. Slowly, slowly, I pulled the bedsheet back and, lying there, beneath the blankets, was a gibbon.

His changes went fast after that, from mammal to reptile, a Galapagos turtle with lazy green flippers, from turtle to toad. We had to keep making accommodations. We put him in a bowl of water. He became a newt, with spots. This is apparently what happens to humans, future and past, backward and forward, young and old, you change and you can't escape it.

Meanwhile, my mother, it appeared, was developing a postpartum depression. "I was obviously too old," she said. "My eggs are obviously no good."

I wanted to say, "hey, what about me, I'm a good egg, aren't I?"

I didn't feel good.

At last, when Charles turned from newt to goldfish, we brought him back to the sea. We three stood at the edge of the sea and my father said, "Let's hold hands. Let's say a prayer," so we did. We tried it. However, none of us could think of a thing to say. The waves were our prayer. They rushed up our feet, foam and bottle caps, crab husks and stink; it was all connected, he'd said.

At last my mother knelt and, using a small kitchen strainer, scooped Charles from his bowl and set him free. He whisked into the ocean without so much as a thank-you. Even though he was so small at this point, we watched him for a long, long time. His orange body glowed like a speck of light that will not leave; it goes on, and on, but it is always distant.

We went home. By the time the cab pulled into our driveway, my cheeks were feeling hot and my mother said, "Sarah, I think you have a fever."

I was a little excited to have a fever. I leaned against the seat, closed my eyes.

"Come in, come in," my mother murmured to me, and she reached into the backseat for my hand. It was such a relief to hold a hand. Her hand. His hand. I walked between my parents back inside our house, up the stairs, and then I lay on the bath mat while she ran me a lukewarm tub.

"Mummy," I said.

"Sweetie, sweetie," she said, helping me in. "My sweet girl, my one and only, Sarah Rose," she said. I let her wash me. I let her bathe my face and neck, pour a cup of coolness

over my hair. I had a strange feeling. I never wanted to leave
this water. When, at last, she had to go cook dinner, I stayed
in the tub. I picked up the washcloth and ran some more
lukewarm. I washed my arms, my stomach. The washcloth
was raspy, rough, I moved it up and down, across my stomach, my shoulders, under my chin, and as I rubbed my skin,
it turned to steam. My skin wouldn't stay. Nothing ever
does. I wanted to cry, but it was too late for that. I couldn't
stop what I was doing. Growing up and growing down. My
skin kept coming off. Underneath, I found my fur.

Ruby Red

... as Snow White grew, she became more and more beautiful, and by the time she was seven years old she was as beautiful as the day and more beautiful than the queen herself. One day, when the queen said to her mirror:

Mirror, mirror, here I stand.
Who is the fairest in the land—

the mirror replied:

You, O queen, are the fairest here,
But Snow White is a thousand times more fair.

The queen gasped, and turned yellow and green with envy. ... Envy and pride grew like weeds in her heart, until she knew no peace by day or night. Finally she sent for a huntsman and said, "Get that child out of my sight. Take her into the forest and kill her and bring me her lungs and liver to prove you've done it." The huntsman obeyed.

—THE BROTHERS GRIMM

*   *   *

I'D LIKE TO TELL my side of the story. So, first off, I wasn't her stepmother. They say stepmother as though that will soften the blow. But it doesn't. It hasn't. It never will. When a woman betrays another woman, it is always, in the end, a mother and a daughter, the primal pair; don't let anyone fool you.

Yes, I was Snow White's mother, and god, how I hate that name. Snow White. Puts me in mind of a petticoat, a pinafore, a candy cane, sweetness runneling down your chinny-chin-chin. I didn't want to call her Snow White. I wanted to call her Ruby Red, because when she was born her lips were a bright pulp slit. They pulled her from me, slippery as a fish, and then they held her up.

She screamed.

"Ruby Red," I thought.

But her father, the king, he said, "What do you think she is, a harlot?" I said, "The name Ruby's making a real comeback, you mark my words," but, being the queen and all, I had very little political power. And besides, I was exhausted. Snow White, or S.W., as I sometimes referred to her in my mind, was my first and only. I didn't conceive until I was thirty-eight. I was, of course, still attractive. I wore long dangly earrings and Indian print skirts. I wasn't sure I wanted a child. I loved being in bare feet, walking long walks in the forest, seeing the different kinds of birds, the names of which I knew, every one. Back then, we didn't have microscopes, this being a completely different century and all, but I did have a piece of old milled glass I'd gotten from the bottom of a bottle, and when I held it up to leaves and dirt it enlarged the small specifics of things, so my sight was keen. I was a woman with questions and ambitions. Why, I wondered, were there gold veins running through a leaf? Was a leaf ensouled, or was it ultimately secular? Why, when you peered into a puddle extremely closely, was it teeming and darting with billions of beings? Who needed to get pregnant? My world was full of miracles and minutiae, and I dreamed of following in the footsteps of someone big, like Galileo.

But what happened, happened; I got pregnant. My feet swelled out. The first time I felt her move within me, I cringed. She was, even back then, so much slither and whisper, so hard to handle, and no matter how much I imagined who my girl might be, her image evaded me.

In those days, even the best of births were awful. I am a petite woman; not in spirit; in spirit I am large and voracious and greedy and good, all of these things together—but in physique I am nothing if not diminutive. My labor started on a moon-fat night. The pains were distant, like ruffles of cramps across my belly in the beginning, and then picking up speed, faster and faster, hurling me to a high place and then heaving me down on the ground again, and again. And the days passed like this. The baby would not come. The king, my husband, waited in his own separate quarters while the midwives and maidens attended to me, bringing me buckets of warm water, massaging my skin with eucalyptus oils, trying to slowly stretch my openings, and still she would not come. This is how it started with S.W. and me. I pushed one way and she sat still, stuck, doing nothing to help, stubborn in the utterly passive way of a woman with great rage and weakness.

THERE WERE rhythms, too many rhythms, and then my water broke. The nurses walked me up and down, up and down, while my cries filled the hallways. "Hush, hush," they said, and still she would not come. The pains came and I had not known the pains. Until they came. Piercing, slithering, sliding, starting high up and then taking me over in waves so total they were almost elegant. And then the undertow, the ebbing away, the harsh defeat, my mouth parched and pinched.

By the third day, I was too weak to go on. And the mid-

wives said the baby would die. "Let her die," I thought. I pictured her inside of me, a tiny dead doll, a hand reaching up
me and plucking her out.

They brought the king in then. This, understand, was
highly unusual, for a man to enter the birthing chambers.
But they brought him in and they said to him, "It's not working. Your baby will die." I looked into my husband's face and
I saw sadness and then anger flit across it, for he wanted a
child; why, I do not know. An heir, a playmate, a lover, what?
WHAT? No one tells me, not even now. He said, kneeling by
me, a royal man with his knees in the menstrual mess, in the
torn clothes and strewn bedsheets, he said, kneeling in this,
a woman's world, "Push, my woman, push." And then he
took my nipples in his fingers and worked them over hard
and perfect, his thumbs understanding just how to tweak
and arouse—we were lovers, after all, and he was always
good in bed, I can't deny him that—he took my two nipples
and then I felt it, like a fist forced open, the baby girl flowing
outward now in a rush of persimmon.

She was born. I lay back on the bed, exhausted. He did
not go to me. No, he went directly to her. If he was disappointed she was not a he, I never saw it, not even for a flicker,
no. He picked the child up. He held her in the moonlight. To
me, she looked like meat, just carved from the big block of

my body. To him, though, I imagine she must have looked like an ornament, as red as Christmas, or like a fairy, perhaps, pupal, with folded wet wings. He lifted her up, high up. He brought her to him. I felt, then, a great gap in my chest, that it was she being brought up close to the king, not I. He was my husband. "Snow White," he whispered. He put his face up against hers and the baby, barely born, the baby latched onto the nipple of his nose and suckled him. I could almost feel his palpable pleasure, a different kind of contraction.

When he finally left, much later, the baby and I were alone. It was a relief. With him in the room, there was simply no space for us to see each other. But now, he was gone. I inspected her closely. I counted ten tiny fingers and toes. I ran my finger around the whorled workings of her ear. I touched her umbilicus, knobby and thick as a piece of raw ginger root. "Ginger," I said. "Ruby," I said. "Rose Red," I said. "Snow White," I said. "What a stupid name."

SHE WAS such an easy baby, such a pleasure in so many ways. I loved her. I really did. I'm not saying that to excuse my later behaviors. I did what I did, I felt what I felt, and I assume my portion of the responsibility. Even my husband had his reasons, though I cannot really find them. Some men love their daughters with a love so large it eclipses reason. I do not exactly understand it, but I can imagine it.

I can imagine many many things. I can see far and wide now, although I am old, and my eyes are marbled.

But she was an easy baby, a gurgler and a smiler, a champion sleeper, and although one part of me liked this, another part of me was uncomfortable. I wanted a girl with some spice and truculence. I wanted a wailer. I wanted a kid with colic who would scream us into a thicket of intimacy, because that's the way I am. I have never liked the dim and the diminutive. She smiled at me so sweetly, how could I not smile back? How could I not feel protective, her skin so thin the veins were visible even in her tiny back? She did not take to my nipple. I have always blamed her father for that. The first suck is the final suck, imprinted.

So, I had to feed her from a wet nurse. I was at once grateful and sad. Grateful because I could hand my sweet bundle off to my maidservants and trek in the forests, which were glorious the autumn of S.W.'s first year, fruit-yellow, merlot-red, the moss dank and private. I enjoyed the freedom. At the same time, my milk took weeks to really dry up. My breasts ached for her, even if my heart did not. My breasts got engorged and purple with pain, and I pressed the cool moss to me, waiting for it to subside.

"Little girl, little girl," I called to her, pressing my milk-smeared fingers to her mouth. By two years of age she was always eager to please, always staring with her wide damp eyes, handing me bobbins and bright pins she found on the floor. We played together and I tried to teach her what was best; I truly did. I tried to teach her a keen curiosity, a healthy dose of selfishness, the gift of grab: *mine.* Bring it to your chest, hold tight. She would offer me her little silver rattle and I'd say, "Shake it hard, kid. Make some noise. Let us know you're here." And sometimes she would. And sometimes I'd look at her and feel pride for the skeins of strength I saw in her, skeins of strength I tried to cultivate. And other times I'd look at her and feel such fear for the flat open sweetness she brought to the world and I'd think, "If anyone hurts her, I'll kill them." And then other times I'd look at her and think, "Did I really birth this boring angel? Who is this stranger, anyway?" I had all these feelings. Everything was a contradiction. This is what it means to be a mother.

I USED TO take her, back when she was a baby, for walks in the woods with me. I'd strap her to my back with strips of silk, and off we'd go. I wanted to teach her the names of all I knew. Meadowlark, monarch, pistil, pupa, my girl should have these things. She should know how to name the world. We spent hours examining the intricacies of stones, the porous bones of a dead bird, the crumpled innards of a peony. I said to her, "A girl should look at everything. She can do whatever she wants."

And we were happy then, the two of us. We were two points joined by a straight line, but when her father entered the picture, it changed. We stretched to a taut triangle then, and I was on the outside, pierced on some point I couldn't understand. Her father, my husband, was a big man who was prone to fits of hypochondria no one knew of but me. In private he'd examine the smallest sproutings of his body with anxiety, but in public, that never came through. He worried about his heart, his weight (he had a little tummy, it's true), the corns and calluses on his elegant feet, the patch of thinning hair on his head. And they say I was vain!

But no one ever saw this side of him. He was a big man, a handsome man, with that movie-star nick in his chin, and a certain ragged edge to his elegance. And S.W. and I, we'd be playing in the sunroom, or up in the nursery, and I'd be teaching her to somersault or to read, and then we'd hear him coming, his footsteps echoing in the stone hallways of our palace, the door swinging open, one black boot, two black boots, the gilt edge of his royal garb; he was before us.

And every time she saw him, it was as though it were the first time. "Papa," she'd cry out, and they would hug and laugh, a ridiculous reunion. He mesmerized her, always. He used his kingly charisma and his masculine strength to capture her in a way I could not. He held her high on his shoulders, so she saw the stars. He lay on his back, and balanced her belly on the broad flanks of his bare feet, and she flew like that, powered by his muscle. She adored his adoration, that's what it was really all about, and his immaturity as well. Papa came to play. Papa tossed and rolled. Mama, on the other hand, Mama put bitter herbs in her mouth when she was sick, checked her bowels every time with a stick, felt her for a fever, and saw that she was clothed. Mama was the administrator, Papa the magician. He pulled pennies from his ears and rabbits from silk swatches, and who could compete with that?

And so we went on like this for years. Snow White was two, Snow White was three, Snow White was ten, eleven, twelve. And then two things happened. Or three, or four, really I'm not sure. Was it that her menses started, and mine stopped? Ho-hum, too predictable, although it happened as a fact. Or was it that he was aging too, and between us, in bed, a kind of lethargy grew, and a dulling of our appetites? No pun intended, the hard plain truth of the matter was this: His plumbing stopped working as well, and this horrified him. I said it didn't matter, but it did. I wondered if it was me, my thinning breasts and hair. He said it was him. He began to visit the province's witch, bringing home herbs and potions, and he took to exercise as well. He was a man obsessed. I have no patience for this sort of thing. I said, "Get over it, buddy, every day is a dying day." Snow White, on the other hand, she was so much sweeter. She knew just what he needed. One day, she sidled up close to him on the couch and said, "Papa, my strong papa." Gag me, please.

Later on, I took Snow White aside. "Listen, sweetie," I said to her, "you shouldn't talk to men like that."

"Why?" she said.

"In general," I said, "talk like that has a low IQ sort of sound."

"I'm just being nice," she said.

Precisely.

OKAY, so I'm a bitch. So I was a perimenopausal bitch, okay, I admit it. I went, then, on a two-month bleed. I bled and bled and then it stopped and there was no more blood and you could say whatever was getting drawn off was no longer, and things festered inside. Snow White, dammit, turned out to be too pretty for her own good. She looked, however, nothing like her pictures in the Brothers Grimm, which is a book no better than a tabloid as far as I'm concerned. The truth is, Snow White's hair was drizzly, as though she'd stuck her finger in a socket, and she took to wearing high heels, and mincing about the palace in them.

She had, at that point, zero intellectual ambitions, and this bothered me most of all. I bought her books on brews and potions, books on the history of witchery, books with marvelous maps in them which showed ancient oceans and crenellated ranges of mountains. He, on the other hand, conspired against me. He bought her unguents and long flowing dresses from the marketplace; he bought her candied fruits to rot her teeth and kohl sticks for her admittedly gorgeous eyes, and ribbons and chaise lounges. He bought her, one day, a glass bed, and this I mark as my turning point. Into the palace it came, carried on the backs of six sweating men, an enormous bed with a soaring canopy of crystal and an opaque headboard. Snow White was so excited; she skittered around like a kitten and later on they both lay back on that bed together. It was evening, and I stood on the threshold to her room as the sun slanted in sideways. The bed glowed. They lay side by side, smug as two chums, and then this: their flanks, just touching.

I got ill. It has to do with hormones, so they now say. Isn't this too simplistic? Who wouldn't have become ill, with a menstruating model of a fourteen-year-old and a hypochondriachal egomaniac to contend with? I developed surges of heat in me; my breasts withered. My skin dried. The heat would wake me in the night, suck me straight from sleep, and I'd lie there, shaking from a fear I could not name. I tried all the acceptable remedies. I visited the witch in her cave, and she put her hands on me, but still, I startled out of sleep, all sweaty. One night, I woke up late, late. The moon was burning by my window. The grasses outside looked phosphorescently green, and supple as snakes. They seemed, those grasses, to be writhing in the wind. And a terrible feeling came over me. I turned in our bed, and he was not there. The house was so quiet. At dinner that night, I had seen them smiling at each other in the candlelight, and let me tell you, Snow White developed a wicked little smile meant as much for me as for him. She wasn't so sweet anymore, but nor was she sharp in a way I could approve of. She was a hussy, plain and simple, a Camille Paglia without the intellect. I wasn't proud.

And I woke up to an empty bed and no man beside me. I stood. I started down the long hallway. The marble floors were achingly cold on my feet. I saw her skirt, tossed in a puddle on the floor. I saw her shoes, the high heels pointing straight up, their noses in the ground. A few feet farther, her shirt, white in the moonlight. And then I stood before her bedroom door. Inside, there were sounds, muffled and indistinct, the swish of sheets, a gasp of pleasure, or was it pain, or was it sleep? I put my hand on her doorknob, the gold doorknob, shaped like a duck's head, that he'd brought her from afar. I wanted to turn it and I didn't. I wanted to see and I didn't. A surge of heat went through me, and when I awoke again, I was back in my bed, and a servant was bringing me an orange, sliced sideways and dripping its juice. Had I been dreaming? Imagining? Wishing? Hating into hallucination? A fairy tale is all of these things; remember that. It's all of these things, but you can't quite dismiss it, because its tale is also true.

This was in a time before Prozac or anything else that might have helped. Not that I would have taken those pills anyway. One day soon after this incident, I grabbed Snow White by a long hank of her hair and pulled her, fast, into the bathroom with me. "Whatever you're doing with your father, stop it," I hissed. She looked at me, aghast. Her eyes were wide. She began to laugh at me then, a low and mocking adolescent laugh that left me entirely without my skin. She stripped me to the quick. She said, "You're sick."

———

WAS I SICK or wise, and where does wisdom intersect with sickness? Was I all-seeing or blinded by envy, or did I dwell somewhere in between these things, in the bland pages of a story I could not comprehend?

IT WAS AFTER the glass bed, the gold duck doorknob, the swishing sheets, it was after these things that my mirror began talking to me. But what the damn fairy tale leaves out is this: It wasn't just my mirror. It was everything! The teacups were talking, there were messages scrawled in the sky, cupped in the navels of the flowers, scripted by the ants as they went on their working way. Mirror, mirror on the wall. Fairest. Fairest. Of them all. In one thousand years and all your fears. Dunking in the washed-out queers.

I had a dream one night, around this time, that I was in labor again, and a tiny child was born to me, a child whose head was so wobbly that the midwives whisked her away. I cried and cried. I said, "Where is the girl I want to love?" and they said, "Any minute now, we will bring her back, let us just screw on her head a little tighter."

It was because I was scared for Snow White that I did

what I did. At least in part. I had to, HAD TO get her out of the house. Just to set the record straight, I certainly never intended to kill her. I admit, I put a little poison in the apple, but let me tell you what that poison was. It was black cohosh, a powerful abortifacient, taken by women who wish to prevent a pregnancy. I sent her out to the forest with my huntsman, and when that didn't work, I told those dwarves to take her, keep her safe. And then, because I feared she was a harlot, because I feared she would get pregnant, because I feared it was her father's baby, because I feared my fear and hate, because I wished to intoxicate her with my own kind of power, the witch's power, the wily power, the woman's power, I stuffed an apple with herbs, dressed up as an old lady (really, I didn't have much dressing to do), and got it to her. The rest is history. She took one bite and fell down as though dead. I knew she'd be fine, though. I knew if she was pregnant the baby would bleed itself out. And if she wasn't pregnant, well, a little bit of witchery never hurt a girl, in the long run. I wanted to poison her with my power, put some hag in her pretty blood. It was a gesture at once loving and horrendous. I am sorry and glad that I did it.

AND YOU KNOW the rest. She fell down as though dead, went to sleep, and eventually got kissed by a prince. She went off with him, all girls do, she made the same mistakes as I. Once, a long, long time ago, when wishing still worked, I fell in love with a man, and married him, and made a home I was never quite comfortable in. This is what women do. We birth our daughters and are replaced by them; we try to hurt them as we protect them, in the most wounding of ways. What the story doesn't say is this: When I gave Snow White that poison apple, I fed it to her like a mother to a baby. I said, "Here, here, little girl," in a cackling voice, and she opened her mouth, and I placed the fruit on the pad of her tongue with gentleness. We touched.

My husband died, of course; incidental characters always do, but I've lived on, for centuries. I seem to be immortal. So is Snow White. She married that prince and bore, god help her, four children, and she didn't speak to me for years. I heard her prince had an affair and she got sciatica. I heard her beauty faded, and her mind grew sharp. And then, one day, in the eighteenth century, I'd say, she came back to me and said, "Mama. Mama." I looked up from my knitting, my eyes faded with time.

"Yes," I said.

"I'm pregnant again," she said, tears runneling down her face. "I'm too old now. I can't do it. I don't want it. I admit it."

I could have given her some cohosh, something to take the child out, but instead I gave her this. "I never wanted you either," I said, and I reached out to touch her wonderful cheek, so she would know that I'd loved her anyway. And we stared at each other for a long, long time, and then Snow White started to laugh. It was a laughter, I think, of relief, to know she was not the only one. I laughed with her. It was the best thing, the only thing I've ever been able to give my girl; a true tale.

We're friends now. I do my fair share of babysitting. I'm helping her remodel her kitchen. When the chaos is too much, and the prince too ineffectual, she comes by my place. We sit in the sunroom together. We say very little, because all has been said, because we speak with our eyes. I understand her now. She understands me. We are both old and ugly. We pass back and forth between us an apple, and on the flanks of the fruit, our big ragged bites.

Defenestration

A MIDDLE-AGED husband and a wife are making love. He is wearing a bowler hat and a starched white shirt and she is completely naked, with two big braids, her head in a pile of pillows. The bed is a big brass bed and the sunlight shines through the open window, which looks onto a field of snow. The husband is working hard and joyfully; the wife, after some time, sneaks a look at her watch. And when she does she is shocked to see both hands skating wildly around and around the silver circumference, while outside the sun has hardened into one dim diamond in a darkening sky. And still he will not stop. And she thinks, as she often does, that any minute it will be over, and that minute is almost worth waiting for, the cramp of his pleasure signaling to her at once the end of an arduous chore and the only certain sweetness they have left between them, as she holds him close, as though he is a tiny child.

But this time, it never happens. He just goes on and on until it hurts her, and finally, her patience worn thin, she says, "Stop!" The sound of her voice, which he has never heard during their thirty-one years of lovemaking, is so unusual, and so exciting, that immediately the man ejaculates.

Afterward, she gets up. She looks out the window. It appears to be neither night nor day, the sun a dim diamond, the moon also out. The woman looks at her watch. It is gone.

She goes downstairs. Everything has changed. The furniture is subtly rearranged. The couches are too far from the wall; the chairs are awkwardly angled. In the kitchen, a small balloon, red as a platelet, hangs high near the ceiling.

In the dining room, the woman finds, on the carpeted floor, a mysterious pile of toy wood pieces. She bends down and sees they snap into place to form a tiny window. She looks around her, and then climbs through the window she has built. Now she is in another world, a miniature world where foghorns echo and people rush past in the rain. Ahead of her, on a cobblestoned street lined with graceful gas lamps, the woman sees white rabbits and umbrellas as colorful and complex as quilts. She walks into this world. The rain is soft and moist. She goes farther and farther into this world until at last she merges with the haze at the horizon.

In his own world, the husband stretches languidly, rises from their bed. Downstairs, he makes himself some tea and toast. In the living room, he sits contently on a couch. He calls his wife's name. In the dining room, he comes upon the miniature window, and thinks nothing of it. He peers through, and, seeing only space, he dismantles the little window, and leaves the pieces in a pile on the floor.

Gretel's Witch

M Y OLD HOUSE wasn't working for me, so I decided to
build a new one. I took an ax and started. My house
was surprisingly easy to dismantle. The white walls cracked,
the ceiling snowed in chunks, and the tan floorboards ripped
up with a rasping sound, like a Band-Aid being torn off
someone's skin.

The neighbors came to me. They said, "What are you
doing, old lady?"

I said, "I am building myself a new house."

They said, "In what style?" and I said, "It is slowly coming clear to me."

I went to the mason yard to pick up stones for a fence.
One by one I brought them back, carrying boulders like the
babies I'd never had, and laid them down.

An inspector walked by and said, "Excuse me, do you

have a permit?" And I said, "I'm through with all that, per-
mits, permissions. You have to live your own life, you know."

The inspector seemed surprised by this reply. He stood at
the edge of the construction, digging in the dirt with the
steel toe of his boot. He said, "My name's Pat Blood."

"Hi, Mr. Blood," I said.

He said, looking me over carefully, in the appraising way
a man studies a woman who might be mentally ill, he said,
"Do you have a husband?"

I said, "Do you know that husband comes from the Latin
husbandere, which means 'to plough a fertile field'? I am not
fertile anymore, and my husband left with a younger
woman."

Pat Blood came up to me. He touched me on the shoulder.
He said, "Can I help?"

"I don't need it," I said, and meanwhile the neighbors
were watching from their windows, faces pressed up
against the glass. Evening came, the treetops dense and dark
above me.

I began, then, to make my new rooms. The kitchen would
be blue, the color of comfort. The living room would have
four fireplaces, one on each wall, so every wall was warm.
The bathrooms would have deep scooped tubs suspended

over small fires perpetually burning, keeping the water hot enough to scald yourself, so the body turns pink and new. I am forty-four. My husband left suddenly and without warning. We have no children between us.

I had the bones of the new house built within hours. Now I could wander in and out, back and forth, through and through, weaving around the brand-new ribs of hardened sugar. A lightness filled me, and when I sang, yellow came from my mouth.

Days, weeks, maybe months went by then. Or maybe it was just a night. I made my walls from real meringue, and when that didn't seem quite tough enough, I switched to gingerbread. I made my windowsills with jelly drops, my floors from candy cane. I slathered fresh frosting for my plaster, and hung the doors on licorice hinges. I used slabs of chocolate for my chimney, I climbed way up and built it brick upon dark brick, and I thought, "From fire to smoke, smoke to air, the distance between something and nothing." I tried, but the math was far beyond me. Some things you cannot figure. Some things you cannot clench. This is the hardest part. Inside my new house, I settled in.

A FEW DAYS LATER, Pat Blood, the building inspector, came by again. He eyed my dwelling; I could see him from my front window, and then I heard him rap at my hard dough door.

"Yes?" I said.

Pat Blood was wearing cowboy boots with red flames prancing up the sides; he was young, too young to be a bureaucrat, I almost told him so. He said, "Your house is not built to code."

"According to my code," I said, and I heard a new aspect to my voice, a sort of surety, the kind that comes from grief, passed partially through.

"May I come in?" he asked.

I let him in.

He measured my walls and picked at the floor. He asked me about my joists, my studs, my roofing material, and the thickness of my wallboard. I said, "Those questions are no longer relevant." He said, "Did you even submit a plot plan?"

"Pat," I said. "May I call you Pat?"

"You may," he said.

And then I stepped toward him, and lifted his hand to my mouth, and sure enough, there was sugar in his skin, and then I lifted my hand to his mouth, and I wondered what flavor, what texture, what temperature. I kissed him then, in my sweet sweet living room, and afterward he held me. He said, "Tell me your first five memories." I told him about the time I'd gone up in an airplane, and seen the pink-streaked sky outside the bubble window. I told him about the little red suitcase I had had as a girl. I told him that my mother made medicines from bitterroot and cohosh, and I recalled the recipes written in ancient script, the herbs hung up in our rafters.

"That's only three," he said.

I searched my mind for more. It felt good to go back, to touch down. I never had a child, but once I was a child. I told him about the heat wave and the horse named Mandy. And like this day passed. From the window I could see the sun hunched on the line of the horizon. Pat left. Yes, a grief passed partially through. I lay silent on my floor. Inside my body something stuttered, stopped. I felt my eggs, dim and dusty now, drop down, disappear. I didn't know that I was waiting. I let everything go.

And it was only then that the children started coming to me. I let everything go. They came out of the woods, like so many deer at sunset. They came with bread crumbs, lost, every one of them, abandoned by you. Or you. *Higgledy pig-*

gledy hot. The witch stirs up her pot. I sat outside. I watched them touch their tongues to my windows and walls. Hansel. Gretel. How my house must have glowed. How they tipped toward me with relief. How I opened myself to them totally, each and every one, pressed the children against me, took them in, and for the first time, felt full.

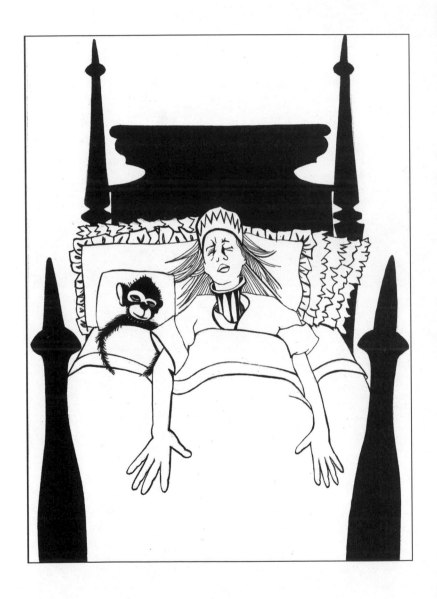

Six Green Bottles

T HERE WAS THIS queen, and she had melancholia. The
king did everything he could think of to make her
happy. He scoured mail-order catalogues, ordered a monkey
and a hummingbird, a dancing dog, an ivory tusk. And still,
she cried. People wanted to know what was wrong. Had she
lost a baby to pneumonia? Had she hurt her back? Did she
not love the king, but instead someone else, someone secret?

"No," the queen said to these questions. "I love the king,
my children are healthy and grown, and my back feels fine,
except for some sciatica." And all the while, as the queen was
saying these things, tears ran out of her eyes.

The truth was, the queen suffered from melancholia,
which means sadness without reason.

The queen had no reason to feel sad, and the very unrea-
sonableness of this situation made her sadder still.

She cried so many tears that eventually the salt and water

grooved channels on either side of her face, and the channels were silvery, and soft.

At night, lying in bed next to the queen, the king touched the channels worn by the tears, and his heart too was heavy. He could do nothing to make the queen happy. He kissed her and touched her face and took her tears right into his mouth as though to swallow her grief away, but it did not work.

And like this they slept, under a sky salted with stars, and a meager little moon, and then, always, the sun, signaling the start of another day.

One summer night, the air-conditioning in the castle broke, and because it was very hot, the king and the queen slept with their windows open. All night long breezes blew into the room, and pink petals too.

When morning came, a strange new sound awakened the queen, a sound from the street, coming now through the wide-open windows.

It was the sound of children laughing, a sound both sentimental and sweet, a sound reminiscent of when her own sons were young, and for just a moment her face brightened before the cloud came over it again.

But the king saw. He said, "You were happy! For just a minute the sound of children laughing made you happy!"

And the queen, rising now, now throwing on her long red robe, said, "This is true."

The king went to his senior magician. He said, "I have figured out a way to make my wife well. I need to give her, as a gift, the most beautiful sounds in the world, so she can listen to them whenever she wants. How can I capture these sounds?"

The senior magician, a very gifted and practical man, said, "What are the most beautiful sounds? First, you have to name them."

"Children laughing," said the king, "and big bells pealing. A river rushing, nuns chanting in a church, the sound of sleeping breath, geese in a cold blue sky, a mother singing."

"In order to capture these sounds," said the magician, "you must go to the source. I will give you a magic bottle for each one of these phenomena. Then you must find a rushing river, nuns chanting in a church, geese in a cold blue sky, big bells pealing, and when you find each most beautiful sound that you have named, put the mouth of the bottle right at the place where you think the sound starts, and then cork the bottle quickly, and the sound will stay preserved in there, and you can give it as a gift to your queen."

So the king went to a river rushing, and he put the bottle

right at the skim of the swift current's froth, and a strange white mist filled the bottle, which he quickly corked, so as to save the sound forever.

He crept down a city street, into a house, found a mother singing, and, crouching behind her so she could not see, he inched the bottle closer and closer to where her mouth was moving, until at last the bottle filled with a pale yellow light, which was the sound of her song, corked in glass.

He repeated this procedure with children laughing, nuns chanting in a church, someone sleeping, geese rising into the sky, and each bottle holding each separate sound filled with a particular color, teal green for the geese, blue for the sleeping breath, a rainbow for the nuns chanting in a church, and when he was done, he brought the lit sounds home to his queen, and he had great hopes.

"I have captured the world's seven most beautiful sounds," he said, "and whenever you are unhappy, all you need to do is uncork a bottle, let a little bit of the light out, and the light will become beautiful noise."

And, indeed, the captured sounds did make the queen quite happy. She sat in the grand master bedroom and let little drops of light out of the bottles, and her ears filled with soothing things, things she had long ago lost faith in—who knows why—but now her faith returned and she recalled that there are, indeed, children who laugh, and breath safe in its own sleep. She grew much improved. She began to play croquet.

Soon, however, the queen could not be without her bottles, for it was the bottles that made her happy. She carried them with her when she played croquet. She took them in buggy rides, and on walks. She brought them into boardrooms, where business was conducted. In the middle of talking to a person, she might suddenly turn, uncork a bottle, let a little drop of light out, and listen, transfixed, and the other person would get offended. People started whispering about the queen, but the queen didn't care. She said, "I could not live without these magic bottles."

Every night, before bed, the queen listened to her bottles, and then she lined them up on the window ledge, where they shone, and her dreams were very vivid.

One night, the air-conditioning broke again, and the king and the queen went to bed, once more, with their window open. A great storm came, and, in a gust of rainy wind, the bottles fell to the floor and cracked open. Out seeped the teal green, the pale yellow of someone's song, the spectrum of the nuns' chant in church, it all seeped out, and melted into the cold stone floor, and then was gone.

"Save those sounds!" yelled the queen. She jumped up and

tried to catch the colors with her hands, and when that didn't work, she brought in glue and pieced the green glass back together, but the bottles, well, even once repaired, the bottles stood with cracks and chips and not a single sound came out.

"What will make me happy, now that my sounds are gone?" the queen said to the king.

Now the queen went to the senior magician and said, "I need more bottles, please." The magician looked at her. He took a good long look. He was a wise and practical man with many years' experience in miracles, and he said, "No."

"No?" said the queen, and she grew frightened.

"Go back to your palace," the magician said, "and close your eyes, and try to remember the sounds, because it is memory, not magic, that brings comfort."

The queen did as she was told. She went back to the palace. She lay on her bed. She closed her eyes. And then came the shakes, the shivers, the sweats, all through the long night, while from deep in her body came cries she had never heard before, each one pitch-perfect and depraved, each one with its own original hue.

The queen did not think she would survive such sound, but she did.

At last, the queen fell asleep, to the original sound of herself. And she dreamt that her neck was glass, her voice box visible inside it, a bright red cube she could open; she did open, to find inside another tiny box, inside of which was another tiny box, each one opening onto the next like rooms in a huge house.

When she awoke the next morning, the queen felt strangely calm. She stood and stared at herself in the mirror. Naked, she saw her hips flared, her neck slender, her two feet sturdy enough to survive. The queen thought her body was a bottle, and even when it broke, it held her.

Swallow a Stone

THERE WAS AN OLD black crow who caught a cold. He had a chest cold which caused him to cough and cough and at last when it didn't get better he went to see the doctor. The doctor listened to his lungs and heart and put the stethoscope on all his pulses and asked the crow to hop on one leg, and the doctor determined there was nothing wrong with this crow, but still the crow coughed. He felt there was something wrong; he had a little stone of sadness in his chest and he could not get rid of it. He pictured this stone sometimes as a pearl and sometimes as a pebble, sometimes as a beautiful and complex jewel, and other times a scraping piece of metal.

The crow had it as a goal to get rid of the sadness by coughing it up. He wanted to see what the sadness was, so he could evaluate it. To that end he went to see a field mouse who specialized in uncommon colds and miseries, and the field mouse gave him a medicine the color of flame. "Take two teaspoons of this a day," the field mouse said, "and we'll get whatever it is out into the open."

Twice a day, then, the crow swallowed the cough medicine. It was delicious and cloying, and he drank it down over a series of days until the bottle was empty. Then the crow crouched down and waited.

Deep in the middle of that night the crow felt something stirring in his chest. He heard rumblings and gurglings, like a great clearing of a throat. He felt a wheezy tightness and then a tickle and then—cough! cough!—he coughed up the stone, which was all of his sadness, and he clasped it in his beak. It is a significant thing, to clasp all of one's sadness, to find in it such a definitive shape, to get a handle on it, so to speak. The stone had in its shadows all the losses of his life— winters where the whiteness stayed so long he stopped believing in the sun. He felt, inside of him, where the stone had been, a lightness, as though he were not a bird but a bubble. For days he floated. The clouds were white as soap suds. The trees were mint-julep green. He went to the field mouse and said, "I've never felt better," and the field mouse said, "Congratulations."

Then, one day, while the crow was weaving in the sky, held high on his happiness, he looked down at the land spread beneath him and saw a bad thing had happened. A whole city was on fire. People screamed, their hair streaming out in flames, the buildings and homes sucked up by tunnels of heat. The crow flew closer and closer and he saw burned people, their flesh hanging off them in strips of char, their eyes melting down their faces. People cried in pain, and then, when the fire was out, people cried in grief, for they had lost everything. "Sing us a song," said the few survivors, who saw the crow tucked up in a tree, and so the crow did. He tried, but all that came from his beak were silly trills, as though he were making light of their tragedy, and the survivors got so insulted they stoned the bird, and he fell down dead.

Years passed. Wind came and cleared the ashes away. In the burned ground, trees took root and grew. The bones of the dead turned to powder, the powder fanned out over the land, and tiny seedlings sprang up, thin blades of grass. Everything decomposed except the crow, who was struck down dead but without death's smell or stiffness. A scientist of the new land came along and found the dead bird and thought it odd he had no pulse but such a supple feel. The scientist brought the bird to his laboratory, where there were many test tubes and bright mixtures of blue and ocean green, and he fed the bird these potions on a tiny silver spoon. Once inside the bird, the potions hardened into a single stone like the kind that catches in your throat when grief descends. The crow opened his eyes. He sat up. He swallowed. The scientist said, "What happened to you, crow, where have you been, what have you seen?" And so the crow told him. With a stone once again caught in his gullet, he sang him a richly textured song of granite, fire, and flesh. And the crow became famous in the land for his amazing artistry, but he was never at peace. He grew very old, and one day a girl of great ambition came to him and said, "I will do anything to have your voice, what must I do to have your voice?" The crow cocked his head, thought for a moment, and then he felt rage. He laughed a harsh laugh. "It is such a stupid, stupid thing," he said.

"What?" she said.

"Great things," he said. "I would advise you against them."

"But what must I do," she said, "if I want to achieve them?"

The crow said, "Have no illusions. You want what you want until you have it."

Still, the girl said, "Give me your voice."

So the crow kissed her, and as he did, he spat the stone into her mouth. She swallowed the stone. And the crow, having twice spit out his innards, now fell down dead and this time could not be revived. As for the girl, her voice stayed exactly the same as it had always been. She tried singing and flute, cello and opera, but she never had the knack. As for the stone, maybe because it didn't belong in her body, it slowly made its way out, down past her heart, eventually into her kidneys, so she passed it. This took years. At the end it was terribly painful. Afterward, she asked the doctor to hold the stone up. "Isn't it a remarkable thing," she said, "to hold in your hand all of someone else's sadness?" The doctor looked at her like she was mad. He placed the stone in her palm. Yes, here she was, holding all of someone else's sadness, as close as one could ever come to closeness. "This," she thought, "is what a life might mean." And when she finally put the stone down, she saw it had left behind on her palm a chalky residue, which, when she touched it to her tongue, tasted of ash and fruit.

The Golden Egg

THE NIGHT is warm, the galaxy visible through my bedroom window. A goose flies in. She alights on my
floor, her tail feathers bobbing, and I can just make out the
curve of a golden egg beneath her backside. The goose
hunches over her egg all night. When the morning comes,
she leaves, and the lone egg wobbles on my floorboards. I
wonder what's inside of it. I figure money, or a man. At last,
with a tiny pair of sewing scissors I crack the egg open. No
money. No man. Inside there is just another, smaller golden
egg, which leads to still another, smaller golden egg, which
leads to still another, smaller golden egg, which leads to still
another, smaller golden egg; it goes on and on; I open them
all, I cannot stop; I keep thinking, "This time—treasure." I
crack and crack, held high on nothing but hope. By the time
I stand up, I have grown old, and am surrounded by shells.

The Gun

WE DON'T KNOW why the men stopped having sex
with us. At first we thought it was each one of us
alone, but then, as time went on, we learned it was a trend.
Our men were aging, stooped, they had long beards and
curved canes and at night they read big books or studied
specimens through their monocles. Hello, we shouted. Hel-
looo. We don't know why the men stopped hearing. When
they were younger men, and we were younger women, their
ears were better, and they heard. Then the town was filled
with the creaking of bedsprings as if crickets were hidden in
all the houses, and the sheets hung on the lines to dry were
spry and white in the wind. Then you could look across a
dark road and see a candle tossing in someone's window, or
find, tucked between two trees in the woods, a jug of red
wine with garlands on the label and a damp cork. That was
then. We don't know why it stopped.

At first we were hurt. We spent time studying ourselves in front of full-length mirrors. We found all the imperfections: the mole, the fat, the yellow. We found some silver in our hair. We put on sweat suits and jogged around the reservoir, the men sitting on benches and studying their books as we went around. We pulled and snipped; we whitened, our smiles turning pure pearl. There were profits to be made from such a situation. Perfume companies proliferated, their scents growing more and more exotic: crushed dahlia, hydrangea, and then the darker scents, like leopard. Fashion designers invented slinky dresses and spray-on stockings. We waxed. The wax was pink and hot and ladies in lab coats ladled it on, let it harden, tore it off, beneath our legs smooth and stinging.

Nothing worked. We don't know why nothing worked. We had been with our men, every one of us, for at least a decade, so maybe it was a question of time. At first we were insulted, but then, we realized, we were relieved. The nights took on a new kind of quality. Our sheets were fresher. We got more sleep. There was no more fumbling with slippery disks and tubes of gel, no more pills in packets, our periods came back, our hormones settled, and we felt, for the first time, normal. We had forgotten what that was like. We got our IUDs removed and we experienced the absence of cop-

per in our bodies. We felt freeer. We had fewer infections. We
no longer ever, ever needed to fake.

Some of us took up gardening. We bought flowers, thick
red roses with hooked thorns, yellow daisies with velvet
navels. The town got green and dense.

We had bridge clubs and swim clubs and we started to
tell each other all our secrets. Now that there was no more
whispering in bed, we whispered in one another's ears; we
grew close; we shared beer late into the night.

We cooked. Without the men around, you would think
we would have cooked less, but no, we cooked more. A cook-
ing craze came over our town, and we made orange-glazed
duck and strudels; we became connoisseurs of cheese, the
blue crumble, the feta, the Gorgonzola. We loved to feel flour
in our hands. We loved the rise of dough. We loved seeing
cream turn to butter, the slow thickening as the whisk went
around and around.

And yes, we grew fat. Not enormously fat, but pleasantly
plump. We didn't try to hide it. We wore short shorts.

We spent long hours shopping for sheets, chambray and
combed cotton and jersey. We were looking to create a certain kind of comfort, or a memory, of mothers tucking us in
at night, our singular skin, the sweep of a headlight on a
cracked wall, when we were girls. When we had long legs

and played cat's cradle and could be as cruel as we were gentle. When our feet were callused from stepping on stones, before our bodies turned. When what scared us were theives and kidnappers and knives, but somehow we felt we were safe. A time before we knew time.

And meanwhile our men sank deeper and deeper into their funks, their intellectual pursuits. We began to wonder what would happen to the human race. We suspected the phenomeon was not limited to our town; we suspected it was worldwide. We suspected younger women were affected too. Because there were far fewer babies. Occasionally we saw one, strapped into the backseat of a speeding car, and it was always an event. *Did you see; a he or she?* We tried to get the license plates but were not able. The cars were always red, and they sped, and they left nothing behind but tire tracks on the road.

Sometimes we tossed pebbles at the men's study windows. Plink! Plink! Plink! They would come to the glass, look out, and not see us because we were so far below, on the lawn, and it was always dark.

We don't know why it happened. Or even when, exactly. It may have been because of the gun. One of us—we won't say who—found a gun in the bushes down by the river. To whom did this belong? Our men were not the violent types;

they were simply lost in study. We studied the gun. It was a golden gun, with a small snout and a trigger curved like a comma. We could see it was full of bullets. The gun felt heavy in our hands, dense, weighty in a way we had not felt for a long time. We laughed and pointed the gun at a tree. We pointed the gun at the sky. We had never seen a gun. How easy to pull that trigger. How easy to curl your finger around that comma and pull back. How quickly death could come, with such a small squeeze.

We fired the gun. It doesn't matter who. In some senses we all fired the gun, although it was held in a single hand. The bullet tore into a tree. Pulped wood and bark went flying. The smell was one of sap and smoke, delicious.

The gun, we think, set something off in us. We liked its kick. We grew restless. We became interested in cars and speed. While our men studied, we careened around the town on two wheels, leaning, right at the edge of something sharp and powerful.

Our bodies began to ache. Our men paid no attention. We swam as fast as possible. We took up carpentry, loud tools, buzz saws and jackhammers, we ripped up our roads. We demolished some houses. We set fire to trash, watching, cheering, as the orange plume spiraled into the air and disappeared.

But no matter how much we did, how fast, how hard, we were also lonely. We had been triggered. Without men, maybe we were becoming men; or maybe, as in any good absence, we were simply forced to see sides of ourselves, as women, that had been there all along. We expanded our repertoire, and yet still, we felt an ache and an unfulfillment. Nights now, our town blazed and smelled of rubble. We ran in groups on the beaches in the evening, our heels pounding the packed sand, the waves suckling themselves, curling in. We felt our fresh sweat, we tasted its tang, and when we were finished we stood beneath sprinklers on one of our lawns, letting this water fall.

And it was there, under those sprinklers, with our clothes plastered or off, that we discovered one another all over again. This was the last thing we did. It took us a long time to get here. We don't know who started it, or if we all just did, moving together as one. We felt skin. We felt breasts, and how they had changed, only to change again. We felt the hollow in our throats, and our imperfect teeth. We felt fulfilled. We fell in love. It was dark. We tumbled on the ground, legs, and lips, absolutely, totally, together.

When we looked up, we could see our men, watching us from the windows. For this they had put down their books. They had set aside their monocles. They were watching us with hunger. At long last their appetites returned, just as we were cultivating those appetites for ourselves. Just when we were doubling. There was something fiery, proprietary, beautiful in our mens' eyes. We stared at them. We stroked each other. We were mournful and exhilarated. We knew this time was over. We watched as the men came toward us, with held-out hands.

The Mermaid

IN THE EIGHTH grade, a mermaid came to our school. Our teacher Mrs. McCray told us about her, how her growth in the womb had gone wrong. According to Mrs. McCray, we all started out with tiny tails, only to lose them sometime in the sixth week, except this girl didn't. What happened: Her feet failed to form, the tail turned trident, and supposedly she was born twitching like a fish.

We'd had special-needs kids in our school before. Once there was a girl with no nose, just a hole in her face; another time there was someone with a lazy eye. But a mermaid? A mermaid! What, exactly, would she look like? Would she be naked on top, her tail silvery with scales? And how would she walk? Would she use a wheelchair? Would she smell like the sea?

Our school was all girls and private, with shaped hedges standing sentry at the entryway, a large marble foyer with a bust of our founder, Miss W. W. Henry. We did Latin and Greek. Lunchtimes were quiet, stately affairs, cucumber sandwiches served with taupe-colored tea.

The mermaid arrived at our school midsemester, on a Tuesday, in late fall. It was beautiful weather, the sky ribbon-blue, the clouds cut out, their edges at once puffy and defined. The mermaid's hair was exactly what you might expect from such a creature, all gold and gloss, falling in wavelets down to the small of her back. On her top half she wore a suede blouse, on her bottom half a long crepey skirt. Her left eyebrow was pierced with a hoop and she leaned on a cane, its handle a blue marble ball. She didn't look thirteen at all. She looked sixteen at least. Instead of two shoes she wore a large single slipper, and when she walked—a walk more shimmy than steps—the slipper swished and the cane clinked.

All of us girls right from the start were afraid and maybe a little in love with our mermaid. Before she came, we were just kids, flat-chested and pale, our lives as laid out as a Latin declension; private school, then Smith or Mount Holyoke, followed by the mandatory professional career combined with two kids and a clean house in some suburb where the streets were named for trees. But after the mermaid came, well, it was as if we realized there were oceans of possibilities opening for us. Sitting next to the mermaid in math class, I smelled her salt, and later, when she left her seat, I found a single strand of her hair, which, when I tasted it, left a tang on my tongue.

Every afternoon, at three P.M., when school let out, all of us girls waited by the back curb for our rides. We were fetched by butlers and nannies and very occasionally a mother with a hard helmet of hair. The mermaid waited with us, but we never saw a car come for her. The last one of us would leave and still she'd be standing there, on the curb in the darkening day, her hair taking on reddish tones as the huge sun set behind the lacrosse fields chalked with white lines.

We wanted to know who the mermaid's parents were. We wondered whether or not she had a boyfriend, where she lived, what TV shows she liked best, and how big her bathtub was. Things like that. She didn't tell us anything. Every day she wore a long skirt. She stood with us, she sat with us, always cool and aloof, her accent in French class perfect.

One day, I told our driver, Tony, to come pick me up late. I said I had a play rehearsal. Then, after school, I crouched behind a boulder and waited as each and every girl got fetched until at last no one was left but the mermaid and me. She didn't know I was there. Her hair pulsed in the late light.

It seemed to be alive. She leaned against the rock I was hiding behind and the strangest thing happened: The rock grew soft against my cheek. She started to sing. I couldn't hear the words, just the voice, and I wanted then, more than anything, really, to reach around the rock and stroke her sea-skin, sing with her, turn myself tail and scale, shedding my thin-girl Latin-loving body for something as unusual and perfect as she. I felt sadness in me, and then the knowledge that someone I had loved a long time ago had died; only that could explain the grief.

At last the light left us completely. Soon Tony would come to get me. He might bring me ice cream in a cone, or a small box of raisins, because he felt sorry for me, an only child, the offspring of parents ambitious and consumed. I stroked the soft rock; I waited and listened. At long last a limousine, black and finned like a fish, with tinted windows and two beaming headlights, drove slowly up the street, pulled to a ponderous stop by the curb. There was the flash of a white-gloved hand as the door swung from the inside. I peered around my rock and in the car's interior I glimpsed crystal decanters, smooth seats. Without a word the mermaid stepped in, and was gone.

AS FOR MY own parents, they were doctors and philanthropists. My father was a plastic surgeon; he worked long hours and had two enormous gold noses as bookends on his study shelf. He also had in his study a massive wooden desk, and a gumball dispenser, which I loved, into which I would slide a nickel and out would pop the biggest, brightest pill, sugary and sweet. As a little girl, I had sat beneath his desk while he worked, every once in a while reaching out to touch his shoe. I chewed the gum, and then stuck the washed-out wads on the bottom of his drawer, my thumbprints drying in them, a sign, *Here I am*. He rarely spoke to me. He read a lot of history in his field. And he was very busy with women whose breasts and bottoms bothered them, or accident victims with faces gone zigzag and bloody. He was famous for his skill, my father. He could take a clubfoot and make it shapely in what amounted, in surgery time, to five seconds flat. Frankly, I think I alarmed him, a child, and a girl at that. Every time he turned around I was growing up and out, my body galloping past his hands. He had wanted, I'm sure, a son.

As for my mother, well, she was a pediatrician and a research scientist, working on a cure for kids' leukemia. Her study, at the opposite end of the house, was filled with pictures of white blood cells. Last year, she was part of a research team that discovered synthetic blood. It was made from people's pus, plus some saline stuff. I remember the day she brought a bottle of it home, and it scared me, not because it was blood but because it was fake.

If it sounds like I didn't love my parents, that's wrong. I loved them to distraction, which was my main problem in life. They were so grand, so successful, so driven and ambitious; I could never compare. Not that I didn't try. I wanted to impress them, especially my father, who seemed alternately bored and repulsed by the girl I was. My attempts were so futile, so stupid. By the age of ten I could play Debussy on our grand piano. I could read Ovid in Greek. I could identify a Caravaggio and a Vermeer, and I could confidently claim the rococo era in art was too excessive for my tastes. I brought home all A's on my report card, except in gym, where I got a B. To all of this my father seemed indifferent.

AFTER THE mermaid came to our school I began to read about mermaids, their history and origins. What shocked me was this: They were not, said one book, descended from humans at all, but from lizards, and they had hearts as red and cold as a reptile's. They could lure sailors into the sea, outsing even a siren, and live forever, drinking froth. One night I read late. I was reading Hans Christian Andersen's tale about the mermaid who fell for a prince and lost her power to love. She gave up the sea; she gave up tail and strength for a landlocked life as someone's wife. Stupid girl she was, I was. I hated myself back then. I turned out the light.

In the dark, then, my father came to me. It happened more the older I got. Evening would pass into blackness; the cars on the street would cease; the lamps would click off, the refrigerator start its midnight hum, and he would come. These were, really, the only times I ever saw him close up. He never hurt me. He certainly never touched me. But he would come and sit on the edge of my bed. He might stare at my ears, or the shape of my eyes, which were wrong, he said, too much almond in them. My shoulders had a hunch he said he could fix; my nose was nice, my lips too thin, and then at other times, as I grew up, not thin enough; he claimed he could reduce them.

That night, the mermaid book beneath my pillow, my father entered my room and something made me want to speak. "Dad?" I said. "Shhhh," he said. He said it sharply, and then he laid his hand on my head, as if to at once shape it and erase it. "Emily, Emily," he said, his voice all clotted, the name not mine.

Then he left. The place on my head where he'd rested his hand hurt. I fell asleep and I dreamt of surgery, of a man standing over a draped body, slitting it sideways, no blood.

THE MERMAID, it turns out, was sassy. She didn't care for rules or success. That made her, of course, only all the more successful, so everything she did seemed excellent. She smoked cigarettes during recess time, standing outside, taunting the teachers by doing it in the open. She point-blank refused to do gym, and no one made her. No one made her! Instead, she sat in the locker room, by the showers, and handed us each our towels when we came out. She'd look us up and down our girl-bodies with a fair bit of mockery. We wondered what was beneath her own clothes. She seemed brave, but she wouldn't take anything off.

One day, in history class, the mermaid set off a small sparkler. Our teacher was Mr. Jones, and all he did was stand at the front of the room and read from a textbook. The mermaid had been in our school about one month then, and we were having to hear about our country's independence. She raised her hand.

"Yes?" said Mr. Jones, looking up surprised from the book.

"I have a question," the mermaid said.

"Yes?" said Mr. Jones.

"Is this book implying that in *your* country"—and here she emphasized the word *your,* like she was from someplace else—"the founding fathers were generous men?"

"They were," said Mr. Jones. "Generous, large-hearted men."

"Fathers," she said. "They're not generous," she said. "They kept slaves, didn't they?"

Mr. Jones looked ruffled. "As was the custom," he said.

"Well," said the mermaid, "that's a pretty fucked-up custom, wouldn't you say?"

Mr. Jones blinked. "Do not use language—" he began.

And then the mermaid did it. "I'll show you independence," she said, and with that she pulled a sparkler from her purse and lit it with her Bic, and a beard of stars fell from the tip to the floor, leaving behind the smell of smoke. I laughed. I wanted something sparkly for myself. I wanted to be able to light a stick, and have the universe flame from its tip. *Here, Dad, watch this.* I laughed, and after class the mermaid, she came to me, at last.

"Cig?" she said, offering me a Camel. We were outside, and it was recess. I looked up into the mermaid's face and saw her eyes, saw, for the first time, that there was something wrong with them. They were oddly flat, veined, and the centers of her pupils were red, as though she had stepped from a bad photograph. "Cig?" she said again, and I shook my head no. The mermaid snorted. She sucked air in through her nose and tossed her head. I could see I'd disappointed her, and I was sorry.

We went into the woods. We had half an hour for recess. We went into the woods, where water streamed over flat rocks; in the treetops birds sang. The leaves closed cathedral over us, and then, when we were standing in shadows, the ground soft beneath our feet, the mermaid said, "Watch this."

She stubbed out her cigarette, grounding it into the earth with her toe. Then, reaching inside her skirt pocket, she pulled out what looked like a fishhook, held it in the light. After a moment she turned her arm up and, using the tip, began to scrape at her skin.

A bird squealed in the treetops. I felt afraid. Small slashes appeared on the mermaid's arm, the blood as dark as mahogany on her ultra-white skin. Around me, I saw the woods were dark. The light filtering through the leaves had an odd quality to it.

The mermaid looked up from her work. "Now you do it to me," she said.

I took the hook. Close up, I could see small specks of rust here and there on it. I lowered it to her arm. When its point struck the skin I flinched back, and then I heard it again, her small dismissive snort. "Rachel, don't be a baby," I thought. I steadied my hand, forced myself forward, and then I began to dig into her. That's what it felt like, digging down into her, and suddenly I couldn't stop; I wanted to get to the cold sea-center of her, where her attitude lived.

"Okay," she said, and I stopped. Blood trickled down. I could see the fringe of her teeth where she bit into her lower lip. She just stood there, holding her cut arm with her other arm, her head hanging, and then, I swear it happened. Could it have happened? The blood evaporated, or did it just dry? How long were we there? The wound looked seamed now, in the shape of an arrow. "God," I said, "an arrow."

The mermaid looked up. "Every cut becomes something," she said. Her voice was creaky. She lifted her sleeve and showed her pink keloid scars in the shapes of swans and lilies.

"You want to try?" she said.

I thought of my father then. I thought about how women came to him because they wanted their marks removed. The idea that I could be imperfect, that beauty might come to me curved and unusual—it filled my throat with hope. Standing so close to the mermaid, I could smell both her brine and her burn. I took the hook, flicked it with my finger, then lowered it to my own arm. The pain came first as a chill and then hot hot, a sensation so pure and true it defined me and refined me both at the same time, so I was living, I was large. I smelled my own skin. It was good.

Afterward, we walked out of the woods together. In the distance we could see our school grounds, the playing fields, the bright swingset. It felt like moving out of a movie theater after a matinee, the world at once flat and harsh. We would go back to class. I would be left with my own little life. But then something happened. The mermaid grabbed my hand, held on to it, hard. "I like you," she said. I smiled.

NOT LONG after that, she invited me over to her house after school. It was all I could have wanted, that invitation. Since the recess in the woods, her desk was the first I looked toward when I came to school each morning, and, in the coatroom, I secretly fingered her sealskin jacket, reaching my hands into the silk pouches to see what I might find: Jumbled bits of shell, a heart-shaped perfume bottle, sand and lint, a sea dollar.

And then she invited me to her house. The long limousine came to pick us up. Even in that car I never saw the driver; he sat behind a pane of tinted glass. The crystal decanters held liquids of every imaginable color, cherry and saffron, turquoise and teal. She poured me a tiny cup of the stuff. "Extracts," she said, and the flavor unfolded on my tongue.

We drove on roads that curled up, hugging hills where treetops were pointed and large birds glided in the sky. We went past all the neighborhoods that were familiar to me, and then into a place I'd never known about before, called Manchester-by-the-Sea. Here, the huge houses were half hidden behind hedges thick and green. The car pulled into a long drive.

The mermaid's house inside: shadowy, elegant, with no trace of parents but a servant to take our coats in the marbled foyer. There were emerald couches and, of course, aquariums built into the walls. The fish had scarlet scales; flabby anemones floated above the pebbled bottoms of tanks.

"Where's your bedroom?" I asked, and the mermaid looked at me, her hooped eyebrow raised, like that was a stupid question. I shrugged. I got that uncomfortable feeling; my body was all wrong; I had too much hip and not enough chest. To my left I saw a curio cabinet displaying sunken treasures, a conch with its inner lip lewd and pink, old coins with a rind of salt still upon them.

We went down hallways then, the mermaid leaning on her cane, her long skirt swish-swishing, until we came to a large open space. Ahead of me I saw a huge indoor swimming pool, its water at the deepest point a holy blue.

Now I saw the mermaid taking off her clothes. She was lifting the bronze clip from her hair so her tresses tumbled down around her face; she was unbuttoning her shirt, telling me to do the same. I did. Her shirt fell away from her shoulders so I saw what was beneath. Her torso was white, white, the nipples the color of melon, the color of carp. Her stomach sloped down smoothly to her waist, and then, when she shrugged off the long skirt and her slipper, I saw at last her tail, or what they called her tail, all supple muscle and stinking of the sea. It didn't look as I'd expected. It wasn't very pretty. I saw what looked like two legs and feet fused together in a mutant mistake, the flesh callused from cuts and burn marks she'd probably done to herself. She appeared to have no vagina, but maybe I missed it, or it was in another place. Without her long skirts on, at last I could also see exactly how she stood, balanced on her pronged trident, like always on tired tippy-toes, only she didn't look tired. Water sucked the sides of the pool. The air was so full of mist the droplets were visible in it. "Go ahead and touch it," she said. I reached out my hand and stroked the tail of a mermaid, like stroking a snake, the living trunk of a tree. She shuddered, and then, a new feeling in me. When it was over we stared at each other, and then fell laughing, uproariously, giddily, into that salted water.

WHEN THE CAR came to take me home, I did not want to leave. I left. It was getting near Christmas. Lights were twinkling in the trees and at home my mother was decorating our tree with balls as bright as hemoglobin. I went past her and into my room. "Rachel?" she called out to me. I didn't answer her. Suddenly I hated her—maybe I always had. I hated her for having me, with my too-wide hips and my sunken chest; I hated her for loving her patients more than she did me; I hated her just generally and hugely, and when I licked my lips, I could taste the pool.

I went into my room, slammed the door. Over the next few weeks I started to see her, and my father, through a scrim, the way the underwater world looks when you wear a face mask and dip below the surface of the sea. It can be blurry and unreal. They began to seem to me—in fact, the whole world began to seem to me—like something staged and virulently untrue, except for the mermaid and me. We alone were true.

I stopped being able to concentrate in my classes. That's because I was always watching, watching and waiting for the mermaid. It had been three weeks since the swimming pool incident. My heart was high up in my throat. One morning I came into homeroom and her seat was empty, her desk at a strange skew. A feeling of dread filled me, like she might be gone, gone for good, and it scared me, not her absence but the effect I saw it might have on me. At home alone, I had taken to standing in front of my full-length mirror and imagining my torso shaped like a tail; I imagined wings on my bare back, jeweled scales on my skin. I could go there. Sometimes, I touched myself. I didn't think of the mermaid then. I thought of forms. Bird, fish, a horse that was half human, a tiger with the mane of a white mare. We could cross over. That was what I thought, what I saw.

And then that day her desk was empty, and when she appeared again, the next day, I knew for the first time the sheer potency of relief. Relief made me bold. After school I went up to her. I took her hand. We went into the woods and she kissed me. I kissed her back.

I got an F on a French test, pop quiz, hadn't studied, first time. I got a B-minus on an English composition paper. None of this worried me, but my father, it was as if he could sense it, could smell it, my sudden saltiness, my swerving from his grasp. During this time, he came to me every night, standing over my bed, saying not a thing, just assessing me, and over dinner, he talked about his cases, clearly for my benefit. "I worked today," he'd say, "on a breast reduction. This woman was so out of proportion a hump had formed on her back, Rachel, and the weight of her own body had pulled her for ward, into a permanent slouch."

I didn't say anything. I spooned up some mashed potatoes.

"Do you know how a reduction is done?" he said to me.

"I don't want to know," I said.

He flinched. Never had I refused his science. Always I had listened as he told me the history of his profession, the history of beauty, twining down through the ages.

"We cut a wedge-shaped slice out of—" he began.

"I'm leaving," I said.

"Rachel," my mother said.

"He's being gross," I said.

And then I left.

After that incident, my father did something strange. He bought me a pair of shoes. They were high-heeled, handsome, and dark. I let him kneel down, slip the shoes on my feet. I felt myself at once lifted and diminished. My bare ankles looked white and wobbly. I could see the blue worm of a vein. My father slipped those shoes on like he owned my legs, and then stood back studying me. "Turn slowly," he said. A rage boiled up in me, but I did it, the part of me that still belonged to him did it, turned slowly so he could see me from every angle. He smiled. "You look good," he said, "like that."

SOMETIMES now, on my own, I cut my arms. I took a razor from the medicine cabinet in our bathroom, and I was surprised by how easy it was. To tell the truth, it didn't even really hurt. The edges were so sharp they slit my skin as though I were made of phyllo dough. At recess, in the woods, I showed the mermaid what I'd done. She seemed vaguely impressed.

I pushed myself, then, to do more, to win her favor. I moved from the razor to a duller knife, which forced me to press down hard into the skin. "Go on, you baby," I'd hiss to myself, "let's see you really do it," and I did.

In school, my grades continued to slip. Maybe slip is the wrong word. They fell, with a loud clumsy clank. Down, down went my French, my Latin, my Greek, every grade a

D, D, for deep, I thought, which is where I was, in deep. Sometimes it scared me; I couldn't recognize who I was or who I was becoming, but I retained a memory of who I'd been before the mermaid, a quiet girl, sane enough, safe enough, I might have even missed her a little. One afternoon, alone in our house, I sat at the piano and tried to play Debussy, but every note sounded sideways, as if the piano were out of tune.

I tried, then, to play something new. Stored inside our embroidered piano bench was all sorts of sheet music, most of it my father's from before he'd become a doctor. He had wanted to be an artist, a painter or a musician, but had chosen medicine in his senior college year. "Plastic surgery," he liked to say, "is the intersection of art and science," but I could see he didn't believe that; it was an excuse. Sometimes I saw him fingering the sheet music, and if he saw me staring at him he'd say, "You play, Rachel. You play."

That day, I reached into the storage bench for a new kind of music. I found, at the very bottom of the pile, old yellowed sheets. It was difficult stuff, choral music from the Middle Ages, heavy and bejeweled, I could do it; I did it, and it scared me, excited me, the sounds I was learning to make. When I finally looked up, the day was darkening, and outside the conservatory window I could see Orion bending his bow in the sky. My father was there, leaning in the doorframe, his pipe crammed with tobacco. I don't know how long he'd been watching, waiting, listening. I looked up and saw him. He stared straight at me. "Ugly," he said, and then he was gone.

ONE AFTERNOON, alone in my bedroom, I slashed my inner arm, just above the wrist, where the skin is papery. The next day, at school, the cut began to bleed again, blotching my white blouse and stinging. I lifted my sleeve, circled my wrist with my thumb and forefinger, squeezed. Blood welled from the wound and ran. I sat there looking at my streaked arm, not quite believing it had come to this, but at the same time, I felt like a fraud, because unless you've tried, you don't know how simple it is to cut yourself. Your skin is thin, it opens easily, and the resulting slashes look dramatic, but really they are just surface scratches. "Excuse me," I said, standing up in the classroom, holding out my runny arm, and the teacher, horrified, sent me to the nurse, who wrapped me in thick gauze. I made up my excuses, a mistake, not a problem, slicing tomatoes and the knife slipped.

Still, the nurse seemed concerned. "What are these other scars?" she asked.

"They're old," I said. "Various childhood accidents."

The nurse narrowed her eyes. I pulled my arm in. "I'm going to make an appointment," she said, "for you to see Dr. Crawford," our school psychologist. Then she stared at me for a long moment before releasing me back to class, my arm big with batting. Walking down that hallway, an emptiness came to me; it came so hard I had to stand back against the wall and close my eyes. Dots danced on my lids. Then there was an ocean in my head, a lot of waves, we could ride them. I thought of how impressed everyone would be when they saw my wrappings. I thought of the time I had ridden high on my father's shoulders, and how simply sweet that was, and how far from that we were. I thought of my mermaid, and it was like we were wrapped up in white together, two mutants beyond the border.

AND SO THINGS WENT. I continued to love the mermaid, and she continued to allow me to love her, but she never invited me to her house again. We kissed most days in the woods, and then after that we would discuss the boys at Middleboro Hill, the brother school neighboring ours. I wanted to know so much about the mermaid: how did she feel about her tail, was it really a tail, or two feet fused together; did she ever think to trade it in for something normal, did her insides ever hurt, was it ever so empty she wanted to bite down hard on a brick or a biscuit or anything, anything, just to taste? I didn't ask her any of these things. The few things she told me about herself only confirmed to me her otherworldly status. She told me her mother had died of a mysterious disease. She told me she'd once loved a boy, named Timothy, who was much older than she, in college. She told me her father had a girlfriend who wore silk pajamas during the day. I thought it was all magnificent. I longed to tell her things about myself, like the time when I was five and a man had lured me into his trailer to take my picture, what my father was like, the gold noses, the plays I hoped to perform. I didn't say anything.

Winter came and went. Snow fell fast, like swarms of moths beneath our street lamps. That was the year a strange left-arm paralysis swept over the entire third and fourth grade, which may be why the nurse forgot about the school psychologist, or the school psychologist forgot about me. There were so many sick girls, so many sick limbs. I memorized the mermaid's schedule, so I could stand at specific spots in the hallway when she walked by. My cuts healed up so fast it was always a disappointment, except for the thin seams of scars with their satiny surfaces, that was nice. "You have nice scars," the mermaid said to me.

To celebrate the spring, and to socialize us appropriately, our school had a coed event in March of that year. This was something our school did every year; the Middleboro Hill boys would come over, and we would have classes with them for a week, just so we would know. Beforehand, the mermaid and I discussed it in the woods. We were both appalled at how all the girls were readying themselves. Nancy Jamison came to class one day and modeled all five dresses she planned to wear, while Gracie Faulkner said she thought blue jeans were better. "Girls," the mermaid said in the woods. "Sycophants,"she said. As the coed week approached, her lifeless eyes did something strange. They became still flatter, and tiny cracks appeared in them. She used her Bic to burn herself.

And then it was Monday of the coed week. The boys came over; the girls were primped and preened, but none of them, of course, looked as lovely as the mermaid, with the hoop in her eyebrow, her long crepey skirts, and her satin slipper. The night before, my mother had come into my room and said, "So what are you going to wear for coed week?" I shrugged, and tried to give a good snort. "What do I care about that?" I said. "Oh, Rachel," my mother said, and she began to flick through my closet, at long last pulling out my most ridiculous maroon pantsuit. "I'm not wearing that!" I yelled, and she smiled then, like she'd proved her point. "I thought you didn't care," she said.

THERE WAS Silas Crocker and Richard Simon and Eddie Gallante and Gabe Buckner, just to name a few. Eating lunch with the boys was the strangest. They had huge helpings of everything in the cafeteria, and when they drank from the little cartons of milk, their mouths had a baby-bird look to them, while, at the same time, a trigger jiggled in their thrown-back throats.

The girls' behavior changed around the boys. On the soccer field, Gracie Faulkner allowed Silas Crocker to score three goals, and I noticed all of our sentences seemed to end in question marks. "Lugubrious means gloomy?" we asked in vocab class. "The mean, the median, and the mode?" we asked in math. As for myself, I kept my mouth shut.

The only unaffected female seemed to be the mermaid— or so we thought. If anything, her power was even more defined. Around her, the boys shoved each other. At recess she stood statuesque in the middle of the playground, held a cigarette between her French-manicured nails, took a slow drag, blew a smoke ring, let the rest waft upward. I over-heard Gabe Buckner say to Eddie Gallante, "Who *is* she?"

For some reason, the way he said it, the way they eyed her, the way she posed for them in public made me angry. "Who *is* she?" the boys kept asking, and finally I said, stand-ing with them by the swing set, "She's a mermaid, duh."

"No way," said Silas.

"Yes way," I said. "Miss McCray told us. It's official."

I couldn't believe I'd opened my mouth, but more surpris-ing to me was the sound, the strength of my voice. It wasn't until I talked to the boys that I realized I really disliked them. Gabe Buckner was handsome, in a hippie sort of way. He had hair down to his shoulders, eyes slender and tapered and sea-glass green. He wore Grateful Dead T-shirts and sang a song called "Ripple" all the time. He himself had something of the ocean in him, something at once liquid and demanding. And he wore a piece of old boat rope for a belt. Since the boys had been around, not once had the mermaid and I walked in the woods together.

"So where's her tail?" asked Buckner. "Well, Gabe," I said, "it's under her skirt. She keeps it hidden."

The boys eyed each other and Crocker started to fake-choke into his fist while Gallante pounded him on the back.

"Show us," said Buckner.

"What do you mean, show you?" I said.

"Go over there now," he said, pointing his chin toward her, "and give it a lift so we can see under."

"I'm not lifting up her skirt," I said. "Fuck you," I said, thinking of the mermaid's words that day in history class. I liked the way it sounded.

"Fuck yourself, lezzie-loo," said Buckner.

"Who's Lezzie Loo?" I said.

"You," crowed Crocker, hooting and pointing at me. I looked down at myself. I was probably the only girl not wearing makeup, the only girl in flat scuffed loafers, the only girl who didn't have on a chunky ring, or a tiny gold cross around her neck.

"I'm not a lezzie," I said, but as soon as the words were out of my mouth, I thought maybe I was.

In a way I betrayed the mermaid by telling the boys about her tail, but it was not nearly the betrayal that she foisted upon me. For the rest of that day the boys whispered and hooted about the anatomy under her skirt, and finally, in the hallway, handsome Gabe Buckner grabbed her cane as she was walking to Latin class. The mermaid tottered, taken by surprise. She put one hand against the wall to steady herself. I'd never seen her need such support before.

"Give me my cane," she said, her voice low. We all stopped to watch.

Buckner slowly, teasingly, held the cane like a carrot out toward her, just beyond her grasp, so she had to lean forward and lose her balance, stumbling a bit, then righting herself again. "Give me my cane, you asshole," she said.

"Here it is," taunted Buckner, and again he held it out to her, forcing her forward, her face going red, her gold hair throbbing, and then, just before she could snatch it in her fist, he flipped up her long skirt, held it high like a tent, and beneath, her mutation, her transformation, the tail like melted legs, the strange smell, all of it.

"Holy shit," shouted Eddie Gallante.

The mermaid grabbed hold of her cane and slapped Gabe Buckner hard on his handsome cheek.

And then the weirdest thing happened. Gabe Buckner just slapped her back. We could see on her scarlet cheek the pale press of his hand.

I rushed up to her then, my mermaid. I couldn't stand to see it. "Lezzies," shouted Silas.

"Stay away from me," the mermaid said, and it took me a second to realize she was talking to me. I backed up. Inside myself I backed way, way up.

The mermaid touched her cheek. She looked so beautiful.

She started to cry. Then Buckner came forward, prince charming, and stroked where he'd hurt, and the sight disgusted me, his hand smoothing, almost sculpting her cheek, the way she submitted to it, allowing her captor to comfort her. After school, I saw them walk into the woods together. "There goes your girlfriend," said Silas to me. That's right. There goes.

WHAT I'VE NEVER told anyone: that day, I followed them into the woods. I stayed at a safe distance, so they wouldn't hear my footsteps. I saw them sit by the stream. I saw Buckner remove tiny white tabs of paper from a camera case and lick them. I saw, from behind my tree, that she licked them too. I heard them, later, begin to laugh.

AFTER THAT, they were together. When coed week ended, I prayed the mermaid would return to me, but she didn't. Now, when we waited on the curb for our rides, it was Buckner who picked her up in his green hoodless car, the tires screeching as they careened around the corner. It broke my heart in half. I mean that. My heart felt halved, like I existed but not by much. At home, half in the mermaid's honor, half to reassure myself, I scratched my arms; I studied my own scars; I saw what scars and clouds have in common: They can take any shape—a lily, an arrow—or no shape at all, just raised smudges on the skin.

The end of the school year approached. The days got that sad balmy feeling of summer and loneliness, of gardens ripening, of days so long they sometimes seemed they would never end. I've always hated heat. As the last day of school approached, I finally gathered my courage and walked up to my mermaid: "You want to come over?" I said.

"Nah," she said, looking quickly at me, then looking away.

"What happened?" I said. We were standing outside then, waiting for our rides.

"Nothing," the mermaid said, and I could tell by her shifting, she wanted only to get rid of me before Buckner came. Suddenly I hated her. "You know, you kissed me first," I said.

"Yeah," she said. "And who'll ever believe that now?"

And it was true. Who would? She looked every bit the lovely lady, leaning on the man's arm, so stylish and proud you could easily not see that every skirt was long to hide her flaw, that she was a creature from someplace else, a creature just visiting our culture, a creature dying to make it her own. I stood there staring at her, and then Buckner zoomed up in his car, and she hopped in, and just before they sped from sight, I saw her turn around and look at me, hold out her cane with its crystal blue ball. "Take it," she said.

"You need it," I said.

"You need it more," she said.

I took it.

And still I felt lost, out of balance. Now that school was out, and she was gone from my life, I thought I should—and could—go back to being the girl I was, the straight-A Latin-loving girl who played Debussy on the piano, the girl who strived for a certain kind of goodness, but it wouldn't work. I no longer wanted my father to ever stand over my bed in the night. I bought a lock for my door. A girl moved in three houses down; her name was Blanche, and she had close-cropped hair and wore cowboy boots, and I admit I wanted to touch her. I admitted it to myself, I mean. At night, lying now behind my clasped door, I thought of a human becoming a horse, the chimerical beauty of certain creatures. One night, when I couldn't sleep, I switched on my light very late and pulled down my Hans Christian Andersen fairy-tale book. I read:

> *The sun was not yet up, as she sighted the Prince's castle and climbed the magnificent marble steps. The moon was shining wonderfully clear. The little mermaid drank the*

sharp burning potion, and it was as if a two-edged sword
pierced through her delicate body—she fainted and lay as
though dead. Then the sun, streaming over the sea, woke
her up, and she felt a sharp pain. But there in front of her
stood the handsome young Prince. He stared at her with
his coal-black eyes, so that she cast down her own—and
saw that her fish's tail had gone and she had the sweetest
little white legs that any young girl could wish for; but she
was quite naked, and so she wrapped herself in her long
flowing hair.

And I felt I understood the story in a new way. It was
about a beautiful, unconventional creature who gave it all up
for a landlocked life. A creature who used pain to conform,
instead of to clarify, or to transform. The Little Mermaid.
She would not be me.

MY FATHER came home one night, and at the dinner table he
talked about a new patient of his, a very old lady who came
to him because she wanted wings. "There's nothing *wrong*
with her," my father said. "She just wants an addition."

"Thomas," my mother said. "The purpose of medicine is
to heal the sick, and that's it."

"I don't know," my father said. Then he turned to me. "What do you think, Rachel?" he said.

"Do it," I said to him. "Give her what she wants." We looked at each other, eye to eye. I think he saw my strength in me. He nodded.

THE NEXT MORNING, I woke up early, very early. The air had the moist high heat of summer. The cicadas creaked in all the trees, and the birds let out their cries. I didn't have a plan. I left our house and walked the mile or so to our town pool. A woman with wings. A two-tailed human. A girl with a girl, the possibilities endless. Ahead of me, I saw the water, the lanes marked off, the slick silver drain down low. A lifeguard was sitting in a high white chair, but other than that, there was no one else there. Inside the locker room, I grabbed a face mask and fins. I put them on. I saw myself in the mirror. The fins were a royal blue, the mask a single oval of clear glass.

I stood, then, alone, at the lip of our town pool, and then I rolled in backward. As the water closed up over my head, I remembered a time, not too long ago, when I had gone scuba diving in the Virgin Islands. I had been with my parents. I had rolled off the big boat, and the instructor was shouting breathe now, breathe now, and I did. And I recalled the shock of being able to breathe beneath the water, how quickly a creature could change from this to that. Or how myriad were the possibilities within a single skin. Perhaps that was it. I could breathe underwater. Now, in this pool, I finned myself forward, skimmed fast along the surface, dove down with my eyes wide open in the water, the face mask fogging from moisture, my hands before my eyes wavering, warping, wonderful, while above me, the air was warm.